Deadly Deception

A Clairemont Island Mystery

by

Vicki Williams

ISBN: 978-0-9876306-3-6 Paperback

ISBN: 978-0-9876306-5-0 Hardcover

ISBN: 978-0-9876306-4-3 eBook

Published: Red Eagle Publications

Editing: Firebird Consulting Editing

Cover Design: GermanCreative

vickiwilliamsauthor.com.au

Dedication

This book is dedicated to the many people who continue to support and encourage me, especially over the sixteen months it took me to write Deadly Deception.

To those of you, who read, edited my drafts, gave me feedback and encouraged me to lose myself in imagination.

Doreen Williams
Michael Young
Veronica Waring
Sarah Mendiratta
Robert Montgomery
Natalie Deane
David Haddon
Gianna De Pra
Lorraine Taine

A very special thanks to my family and friends, you have always believed in me, and support all my writing projects. Your loving support and encouragement are welcomed with open arms regardless of the distance.

CHAPTER ONE

Suffocating In Life

The South Pacific boasts of many beautiful things, but none more so than the remote and picturesque Clairemont Island. Famous for its unprecedented views, tourists flock there in droves—and residents wait with bated breath for their chance to escape its clutches.

In a crowded room in the Clairemont Medical Centre Dwayne Olsen lay in a tiny hospital bed, annoyed that the heart attack hadn't killed him. He wondered what he was going to do with his life, now that he'd been spared the clutches of death. On one hand, he was grateful to be alive, but on the other, he hated his life so much he didn't want to carry on this way. Something had to change, but he didn't know what, or how to go about fixing it.

Confiding in a sympathetic nurse, Dwayne described his life as suffocating in a loveless marriage and dead-end job. He struggled every day to get up out of bed and face the world.

He watched with interest the other patients in the tiny shared hospital room; he was particularly intrigued when their families arrived to visit—the loving embrace of husband and wife and the excited chatter amongst children.

Susan, Dwayne's wife of eighteen years, and their only daughter, Emily, came to visit. They had seemed genuinely concerned for his health and wellbeing, but lying there in bed, watching the interaction with the other patients and their families, Dwayne realised what his problem was.

The spark had gone out of his marriage. There was a definite distance and disconnection in their relationship. He wasn't sure what had happened or when it started going downhill. All he knew was that he was unhappy in his marriage.

It dawned on him that his life was pretty miserable. He would come home in a foul mood after a frustrating day at work. Susan worked late most nights and, if she was home, she would be on the phone or doing paperwork she had brought from the office. Emily, their only daughter, would always be in her room, doing homework until called for dinner, and would retreat back to her room immediately after eating.

Dwayne reflected on his pathetic life: he identified his interests as being football and work. They used to give him lots of satisfaction, but over the last few years he had lost interest in both of them. The football season was finished for the year and he was seriously thinking that he had done his dash and that, thanks to his heart attack, he might not be able to coach the coming season.

Internally trying to process what he felt about his

marriage, he saw himself as standing still whilst life passed him by—as being left behind and forgotten about. This was certainly the case with work and with his daughter. Emily, a beautiful, sweet, soft-spoken girl, the spitting image of her mother. In fact, Dwayne had often wondered if he had anything to do with her creation: she was an angel in disguise. The best thing that had come out of their marriage, he would do anything for her, but the teenage years had seen their relationship take a serious turn for the worse. Emily had stopped talking to her father years earlier—his failure to connect on a level he couldn't comprehend had left them virtually as strangers.

The day before Dwayne was discharged, Kathy and Simon O'Connor visited him. Kathy and her husband Simon were Dwayne's only real friends; they had all gone to school together. Dwayne and Kathy worked together at Clairemont Supermarket, he as the bookkeeper and Kathy as the admin officer.

Kathy knew Dwayne had grown to detest his job; his frustration became more apparent every week. He was a very private person, and therefore Kathy was taken aback when he admitted how he felt about his home life.

They spent hours that night in the Medical Centre brainstorming possible job prospects. The island didn't offer much advancement in his line of work, unless he was willing to start his own business. Whilst admitting he wasn't sure he had the skill set to carry off running his own business, he succumbed to seriously thinking about it.

Most bookkeeping positions were on the mainland. The commute put him off more than anything, although, if necessary, he could move to the mainland, but was he ready for that? Kathy was the one to bring up the possibility that a move might help put his relationship with his wife and daughter into perspective. Susan had a thriving real estate business and was well respected on the island.

Emily, fourteen and a diligent scholar, was getting straight A's, so moving her with only a few more years of schooling would be a terrible mistake, unless there was no other option.

Kathy looked at Dwayne with a different set of eyes, now aware of how desperate he was to make life changes. This heart attack had given him lots to think about.

Gabby Saintclaire, manager of Clairemont Resort, poked her head in at the door of Dwayne's shared room.

"Hello, Dwayne. I heard you were in here, are you OK? I trust you are being well looked after, but if you need anything please let me know." And with that she was gone.

Dwayne looked at Kathy who was laughing to herself.

"What's so funny?" he asked.

"It's Gabby—she's like a magical ray of sunshine. I reckon she knows everything that's happening on the island and she'll appear like this, poof, and then she's gone again, but while she's here for that split second, she'll have updated herself on everything happening around her, sometimes I wonder how she does it."

"You have to remember that she spent years on the police force, so she's trained to obtain information without you realising she's doing it, that's a gift

4

she'll never lose. Shame she quit the force though, a real shame."

The story of Gabby's arrival to Clairemont Island five years earlier was common knowledge. A Sydney police officer, she was injured in the line of duty; far too active to be desk bound she opted for a career and lifestyle change. The opportunity to manage Clairemont Resort came quite by chance, but under the assurance of her husband, Michael, she accepted, knowing the change of scenery would do her the world of good. She was so pleased she did, but old habits certainly died hard.

"Enough about Gabby, when was the last time you went out and enjoyed yourself?" Kathy asked.

"It's been years since Susan and I last went out. In fact, I think it was with you guys at last year's New Year's Eve party at the resort."

"Well, then I reckon it would be a good idea for you to go out, without Susan. We have been invited to a party on Saturday night at Lenni's place, come with us. If one of Lenni's parties can't get you to reinvigorate your life, you're pretty much screwed," replied Kathy.

The doctors had identified stress as being a contributing factor that helped cause his heart attack. Dwayne was discharged from the Medical Centre the next day, knowing his life would never be the same again. There were two changes he was going to make—there was no going back now that he'd made the decision.

He was going to quit his job and make changes in his home life, whatever that turned out to be. He just didn't know when or how it was going to happen.

CHAPTER TWO

Signed, Sealed And Delivered

Grant Woodham enjoyed working for Coastal Developments. He was one of the original contractors to bid for the billion-dollar project on Clairemont Island. His first visit to the Island met with considerable challenges. The Coastal Developments board of directors was only interested in one thing, making money, lots of money!

When Grant learned that Lenni Maxwell, the famous musician, had a home on the island, it didn't take a rocket scientist to see the potential for making a healthy profit from this investment. Lenni had a fan club of millions; once the fans learned affordable property was available within walking distance to Lenni's estate, these condos would sell like hot cakes.

Lenni's mansion sat nestled upon one of the mountain ranges. Not many people knew that Lenni lived on Clairemont Island, but Grant was more than willing to leak it to the media, at just the right time.

When Grant approached Lenni about the project he seemed thrilled with the idea, he could see the potential, but recently Lenni had been avoiding his calls, and Grant needed to know what was going on —or rather the board of directors had told him in no uncertain terms to get Lenni on board, no matter what it took.

Time was against them now and they needed this deal to be settled before the council got wind of what was really going on.

As a guest at Clairemont Resort, Grant suggested Lenni meet him for dinner at the Glasstop Restaurant. He was on a tight schedule and needed to get back to the mainland before the impending cyclone hit the Island and stopped the ferries.

Grant had only met Lenni a few times. He wasn't a fan of his music. Listening to him over the phone filled Grant with a feeling of dread. It was hard to pinpoint why he loathed this man. Was he jealous of his fame and fortune, or was there more to it?

He didn't care—he was hired to do a job and he'd dealt with this type of imbecile before.

Lenni was late in arriving, which seemed to annoy Grant even more. The meeting didn't go well. Lenni was getting cold feet; he liked the idea, but he'd heard whispers about the project. Although he didn't have any concrete evidence, his gut told him to get out now, before it was too late.

Grant Woodham was furious. He stormed out of the restaurant after Lenni, eventually catching up with him in the parking lot. "How dare you pull out now, this contract is signed, sealed and delivered, you can't do that," Grant asserted categorically.

"Sorry mate, I can do what I like, and this deal is

not for me. I've heard rumours about it and I don't want to be a part of it anymore: end of story."

Lenni reaffirmed his position by climbing into his car and closing the door.

Grant recalled the conversation with the Coastal Developments board of directors: "Get Lenni on board no matter what!"

He took a moment to think about his next step. They needed Lenni. If he was part of the marketing, they would all make millions. If he wasn't part of the project it would still be a success, but only marginally. Undeniably, it would cost Grant his job, and was he really ready to give all this up? Deep in his heart he wasn't entirely sure.

CHAPTER THREE

What Are You Hiding?

"Hey Troy, long time no see, what brings you to Clairemont Resort?"

"G'day, Andrew, what's it been, five, six years since we last saw each other?"

"It's been eight years since I left Melbourne Law School and went to Manila. I worked the bar at Raffles Hotel until I came here to a friend's wedding and knew this is where I wanted to settle. What brings you here, business or pleasure?"

"Pleasure, actually. Mum and Dad have invited my sister Rose and me to celebrate our new jobs. Rose is heading back to Hong Kong and I've just been offered an extraordinary opportunity in New York, so this may be the last time we're all together. They don't arrive until tomorrow, so I thought I'd come over early to chill out before I have to put on a false persona." Andrew looked at his old uni friend with shocked bewilderment,

"What do you mean, put on a false persona? I

don't understand."

"It's a long story," muttered Troy.

Troy Anderson hadn't changed much since they were in uni together; he was still sporting the same Tom Cruise type haircut, his smoky blue eyes added to his sexy demeanour. Having just turned thirty, Troy stood almost 186 cm. He was very athletic looking, his chiseled beard of fine stubble and moustache was the look these days—ever since Ryan Gosling hit the magazine covers. Most men that age wanted to resemble the latest sex symbol, and most women loved the look.

"Let me serve that couple over there, then I'll grab the two of us a drink and let's catch up, OK?"

Troy nodded in agreement. Obviously, things had happened for Troy to be worried about the meeting with his parents thought Andrew, as he made his way to the other end of the Zanzabar and proceeded to greet the couple who had just walked in.

Andrew Graham had worked at the Clairemont Resort for six years; he'd just been promoted to bar manager and for the first time felt his life was finally on track.

The couple from Canada was deep in conversation. Andrew was to learn they were on their honeymoon. Realising they wanted to be by themselves, Andrew served their champagne and the cheese platter they requested, then poured a pint of beer for Troy and Pepsi for himself.

With drinks in hand, Andrew made his way back to Troy. "OK mate, spill. What do you mean you have to put on a false persona? I don't understand; you used to like your parents and sister, so what's happened?" Andrew asked apprehensively.

"Don't get me wrong, Andrew, I like them. They're amazing at what they do, and I adore my sister, Rose, but I don't know how much longer I can take their outrageously high expectations of me. Honestly, they think I'm the squeaky-clean kid that I was way back at high school. I haven't been that person for so long I don't even know how to be him anymore. I'm so scared of being with them this weekend that I almost didn't come.

"I don't want to disappoint them, but I'm scared to death I'll slip up and they'll see me for who I really am, and that would destroy them," choked Troy.

As Andrew poured a second round of drinks, he checked in with the honeymooners who were content enjoying each other's company.

"From what I can remember, your parents were pretty open and forward thinking, they're both successful medical practitioners aren't they?" asked Andrew.

"Yeah. Mum is trying to slow down her gynae practice, but unfortunately the more she tries to slow down, the more women, older career women, want to start their families. And the older the woman, the more at risk they are, which keeps Mum really busy."

"Dad, umm—" Troy paused a moment as he took a refreshing mouthful of beer. "Dad will never slow down, he lives for his work, always has, always will. Thankfully, society is focused on the perfect face, the perfect body, making his plastic surgery business one of the most lucrative practices in Australia.

"Because they are so successful they expect nothing less from Rose and me. Now that Rose, a dentist, has secured a job in a prestigious Hong Kong dental clinic, the pressure is really on.

"The fact that Dad paved the way for her to get this job doesn't for one moment indicate that Rose isn't competent enough for the position; I'm more than certain she is excellent at what she does.

"He's done the same for me—used his connections to get me into an associate role in a law firm in New York. Don't get me wrong, I'm really grateful, but if anyone found out about the real me I'd go down like a ball of flames, my reputation would be shot and my family would disown me."

As Andrew looked around the bar he was disappointed to see a large group walk in. Bad timing, he thought to himself.

"Things can't be that bad, surely?" Andrew tried desperately to reassure his friend, but sensed there was something else going on, something on a much deeper level.

"You don't know the half of it," whispered Troy under his breath.

Andrew attended to the needs of the group of middle-aged businessmen who had just entered the Zanzabar.

Pangs of dissatisfaction flooded him as he remembered just how much he and Troy had lived it up during their years at university, and just how much he had lost as a result. It was because of Troy that Andrew had been asked to leave Melbourne Law School before he'd completed his undergraduate qualification. This feeling of anger had always simmered in the pit of his stomach, festering. Today though, seeing Troy and hearing of his accomplishments only made him angrier.

Andrew kept trying to shrug off waves of anger. An associate position, how in the hell had his father managed that? It sure as hell wasn't Troy's grades that secured him the job. At university Troy was lucky to scrape through each year, he remembered that much.

Glancing around the bar, Andrew couldn't help, but wonder what dirty little secrets Troy was hiding —what was he so afraid of sharing—what would be so bad that he could destroy the relationship with his parents, lose his job and tarnish his reputation? He shuddered to think.

As more guests entered Zanzabar, Andrew knew he would not have the opportunity to ask Troy what had happened over those years. Troy's parents would arrive the next day and, as Troy had said earlier, he would have to put on a false persona. Troy would have to delve deep into his memory bank to retrieve that squeaky-clean kid that his parents believed him to be.

An hour later Andrew noticed Troy slip quietly away; he wondered if he was heading to his room or to somewhere else on the island.

Whatever Troy had been up to intrigued him deeply.

CHAPTER FOUR

Exotic Beauty

Troy was woken with the repetitive knocking on his hotel room door.

" H o u s e k e e p i n g " — k n o c k — k n o c k —"housekeeping," announced a young woman.

A few minutes passed before he registered what was happening. He bounced out of bed, totally naked as he reached for his jeans lying on the bedroom floor.

At that moment the hotel room door opened and his eyes were drawn to a stunningly beautiful young woman—olive complexion, long dark brown hair tied in a ponytail. As she turned to face him he noticed her high cheekbones, the luscious full lips, and the sensual brown eyes that framed her face perfectly; and the body! She had a body to die for, perfectly proportioned with very welcoming perky breasts.

Ah, yes! She was a welcome sight this early in the day.

Lucille Peyton-Smith, unaware the room was occupied, looked up as she pushed the cleaning trolley further into the room. As their eyes met Lucy, as her friends called her, went a deep shade of red.

"Oh my god, I'm so sorry," she said as her hand instinctively shot up to cover her eyes.

"Please forgive me, I'm sorry for barging in, I didn't think anyone was here. I'll come back later to clean."

Attracted by her beauty, Troy realised he was still standing buck naked, only now he was aware of the massive erection the sight of her had aroused in him.

Turning quickly, he hoped she had not noticed his erection, but in the same breath, he hoped she had. His desire to have her was evident.

"It's time I was up anyway. Please go ahead and clean. I'll have a quick shower if you want to start cleaning here first." He gestured toward the kitchen area as he backed into the bathroom, jeans covering his private parts.

Troy closed the bathroom door and stepped into the shower. Not waiting for the water to warm up, he enjoyed the cascading water as he quickly cleansed his body. He would normally take ages in the shower, but today, not wanting to hold the cleaner up, he performed his cleansing routine with considerable urgency.

When he emerged from the bathroom, draped in a thick fluffy white towel tied around his waist, Lucy couldn't help but notice his muscular, toned body. She could tell he looked after himself; his abs couldn't look that good without a regular workout.

Experience had taught her how to keep her body looking great. She hoped and prayed she would always be financial enough to keep her looks her number one priority, knowing full well her body was going to be her saviour. Her looks and body were going to take her places: one day she would escape this god-forsaken island.

For an instant she was taken back to her youth. She had had a hunger for intimacy, thinking naively that her body would bring a loving companion, someone who could take her away from this island and into the life she had only dreamed about. Her dream of being a model and escaping the island was intense.

In reality, all her body beckoned was the lust of teenage boys whose intentions were not of a loving nature. They were just seeking a reputation for banging the most beautiful girl on the island.

It didn't take long for Lucy to use up all the eligible males on the island. Her hunger to feed her dream was sustained when she realised young businessmen attending conferences were the ideal candidates. She had long known that men, married or not, were fair game when she was around.

Lucy begged the human resource manager at Clairemont Resort to give her a job, and then set out to target worthy participants, of whom there were many.

It wasn't long before Lucy revealed her pregnancy to her parents. Aware of her reputation on the island as being *very easy*, and not knowing who the father of the baby was, her parents decided to teach her a lesson and refused to fund her desire for an abortion.

"Lucy, you sleep with the devil, now you live with the devil's spawn," her mother spat the words as her father just shrugged his shoulders, totally non-committal.

Ill-equipped and lacking the maturity to care for a baby, Lucy was thrilled when her father up and left: one day he just didn't come home. Divorce papers arrived a week later. Lucy saw this as an opportunity, a blessing in disguise; she knew the first part of her escape was taking effect. She begged her mother to let her go back to work. She was, after all, struggling to bond with and care for the bastard baby she didn't want, and she could earn more in tips than her mother made in a year. Thankfully, the resort agreed to her returning from maternity leave early.

The sight of Troy, and yes, she had caught sight of his erect penis, had started a yearning she hadn't felt in quite some time. Since she had been back at work there hadn't been a guest that turned her on like this. She was sick of banging stuffy, old, fat men just because they tipped well and showed her loads of attention.

Here, standing in front of her, was a beautiful specimen. As her yearning kicked into gear she was drawn back to her dream of getting off the island, starting a new life—anywhere, but here.

Casually she asked if he was here for business or pleasure.

"Family vacation before I start my new job," Troy responded, aware that he shouldn't get too friendly with the help, but at the same time he enjoyed the close proximity that allowed him to bask in the presence of her beauty.

"New job, ah! That sounds interesting, what's the new job?" she questioned.

"I'm a lawyer and have just secured an associate position in a law firm in New York."

Cha ching, cha ching, dollar signs rang out loud and clear. A lawyer with a body to die for, this guy was certainly worth pursuing.

"Good luck with the new job and I hope you have a great vacation on Clairemont Island. I've lived here all my life so if you want a tour guide let me know and I'll make it happen. My name's Lucy, by the way."

As she walked past Troy she accidentally brushed against him, knocking the towel from his waist. When it fell to the floor, Lucy instinctively bent to pick it up, only to be met by the rising engorgement of a desire deep within his loins. Without a second thought, he asked if she saw anything she may be interested in.

Her response of *hell yeah!* was all he needed as he carried her to the bed.

CHAPTER FIVE

Expectations

There was a swing in his step as Troy carelessly made his way to the Glasstop Restaurant at the Resort. His parents and sister had arrived and what was once a depressing thought was now not such a big deal. He had dreaded seeing his parents; their high expectation of him usually didn't take long to anger him, leaving a taste of disdain.

But today, after making love to Lucy, he felt content. She had expertly moved around his body, meeting every one of his needs, a perfect match made in heaven; this was the motive behind his smile. He knew he was going to see Lucy later that night, as she had invited him to a party on the island. He couldn't wait to see her again; the thought of making love to her was almost unbearable.

All he had to do was get his dutiful meetings with his parents out of the way, and a round of golf with his father, which he was actually looking forward to.

On the golf course, they were regarded as equal; the atmosphere was always more relaxed when they played golf.

Troy noticed his mother immediately; there was no way of ignoring the immaculate presence she projected. Everything about her was perfectly contained as an illusion for the world to see. Only those close to her knew the manipulative controlling woman she really was.

But as her presence commanded respect Troy remembered only too well how he was to behave around her, and he reverted into the passive puppy dog persona he had lived through childhood.

Thankfully, his sister Rose picked up on his hesitation to approach the table and quickly moved forward, kissing him on both cheeks, melting his apprehension immediately. He loved how Rose was very intuitive when it came to him.

Stan and Rita Anderson rose from their chairs to greet their son. Once the pleasantries were done, they introduced Troy to their other guests including Gabrielle and Michael Saintclaire, managers of Clairemont Resort. Troy took his seat and proceeded to get acquainted.

Rose, a chatty popular socialite, had learned well from her mother. Rita had taught her to command a presence in the room, how to attract and solicit conversation from absolutely anyone. It didn't matter who you were, Rose could engage you in intimate conversation within minutes, leaving you with a feeling of being long lost friends. He loved that about Rose. She was certainly in her element today, capturing the attention of the men at the table.

Rita had come from money; her family was into real estate, not your common real estate, but specialised in the million-dollar properties. The commission on one of those properties equated almost to Troy's annual income. That was until now. This new position with a reputable law firm in New York would bring about a hefty pay rise, and he was looking forward to that. He desperately needed the additional income to sustain his lifestyle. The move in itself was going to cost a small fortune, but for all intents and purposes this was the best outcome, regardless of the fact daddy dearest had called in a multitude of favours to finalise the deal.

Troy just wasn't too sure exactly who he was to be indebted to, and what the unspoken payment was to be. I suppose I'll find out eventually, he thought to himself.

They chatted amicably through the entrée then Stan stood to toast to the success of his children. Troy, realising this was going to take a long time, helped himself to another glass of wine; he offered to top up Gabrielle's glass—she declined by whispering that she was still on duty.

Stan Anderson didn't say much as a whole, but when he was passionate about something there was no stopping him, and the success of his children was his number one priority.

As Troy watched with interest the intimate interaction between mother and daughter, he was pleased that Rose had developed her own striking features, even if they were at the hands of a professional. As a child, she was the spitting image of her mother. Troy sensed that, although Rose loved her mother dearly, she didn't want to be constantly reminded of her every time she looked in the mirror. She didn't call upon her father, but instead confided in one of her father's good friends, one that Rose trusted and respected enough to give him full access to her body in more ways than one.

Lunch served, success celebrated, Gabrielle and Michael Saintclaire slowly made their way around the table, saying their goodbyes as they retreated back to work.

Troy excused himself to use the bathroom. Upon his return he chose to sit next to Rose. He had only spoken to her briefly when he arrived.

His mission today was to get a more recent photo of them, as the one he carried in his wallet was ripped and torn. It portrayed her in days long gone, the smile that would melt your heart oozed from the piece of paper that warmed his most troublesome nights.

Taken when Rose was a teenager, complete with braces, she was a looker way back then and still was today. His priority was to get a photo taken so he could remember her just like this, forever. The braces had certainly paid off, and posed an asset in her profession, but then he couldn't remember any dentist who didn't have perfect teeth.

Like two peas in a pod, Rose and Troy shared similar interests except for academia. Troy was too interested in the social life while at university. It had always troubled Rose how he had graduated Melbourne Law School with excellent results, knowing how little he studied and how hard he partied. Maybe he's more intelligent than I give him credit for, she thought.

University for Rose had not been easy. She

struggled at the start to study, but it was being away from her family that was the most debilitating for her. Just eight hours flight from home, The University of Hong Kong was the best that money could buy. She had the grades, had the passion, and had the family finances to back her dream. Her focus was straight A's and she wasn't disappointed. She sacrificed a lot over those years, but now she had the perfect job and perfect lifestyle. It had all paid off, or so it seemed.

Listening intently, Troy struggled to keep up with the conversation; he was secretly perplexed by the sensual pursuit of the morning. Why couldn't he get Lucy out of his mind? Apart from her body, what beckoned him to her, what magical power did she possess that haunted his every thought? The more he thought of her, the more he wanted her. He couldn't wait until this evening—he wasn't at all interested in attending the party. He wondered how committed Lucy was to attending; maybe he could talk her into returning to his room to make love all night instead.

Stan, signing the tab, looked over at his son and asked if he was ready to hit the golf course. "Just a quick stop to the bathroom and I'm all yours." Troy realised the wine was taking effect.

It was a beautiful day out, the cool breeze and spring sun was refreshing on the skin, not too hot, just right, thought Stan as he teed off. Troy, a little apprehensive at first, didn't take long to get into the swing of it and become at one with his clubs. The afternoon was lost in the eighteen holes; father and son enjoyed each other's company and were totally absorbed in the conversation of golf. Nothing else mattered to them; out there on the green, they didn't take score, they were in a world of their own.

They parted company only briefly as they went back to their respective rooms to change for dinner. Troy was more comfortable now around his parents, it always took him a while to warm up to them after they'd been apart for a long period of time. It had been almost a year since he'd made it home to Sydney, and the only reason he returned to his hometown was to mend his broken heart.

His girlfriend of two years had run off with one of his best friends, leaving him devastated. Deciding to put some distance between them, Troy chose to go home for Christmas and spend some quality time with his family. He knew Rose would be there—it was always easier when Rose was there to be the buffer between them all.

Walking into his hotel room he tried desperately not to think about this morning. He was there to shower and change for dinner, not get lost in thoughts of the exquisite olive beauty he'd had for breakfast.

CHAPTER SIX

Step Into The Future

The Glasstop Restaurant is situated in the middle of the Clairemont Resort complex; its name came about because of the glass roofline that majestically made guests feel at one with nature. Outside, the mass planting of evergreens with lush green foliage, mixed with deciduous trees, created a warm and inviting canopy all year round. The large bi-fold doors at the far end of the restaurant were a welcome addition—when fully opened they allowed guests to sit on the balcony and still feel part of the luxurious atmosphere emitted by the restaurant.

Jennifer Robins, seated with a group of guests attending the *Step into the Future* conference, was quietly getting to know the ladies either side of her while they were waiting for their drinks to arrive.

She had decided to attend even after Sarah, her university colleague, had pulled out at the last moment. Sarah had suggested the conference to Jennifer and, after reading the program event schedule, they knew they would get maximum benefit from the key speakers and topics covered. They booked in for a week, even though the conference was only for the weekend. In need of a break from their hectic university semester, the two academics were looking forward to a week of rest, relaxation, massages, with plenty of wine and pampering.

Sarah, unfortunately, had a family emergency. As she was leaving for the airport, her husband was rushed to hospital as a result of a workplace accident.

As Jennifer glanced around the room she noticed only a few empty tables; she had overheard some guests say the resort was unusually busy for this time of the year, regardless of the imminent arrival of the cyclone heading for the island.

While they waited for their lunch to be served Jennifer excused herself to visit the bathroom. The service was extremely slow; she wasn't sure if that was normal for the restaurant or because it was incredibly busy. It was 1:00 p.m. and Jennifer was starving.

Oh, how she missed Sarah. She totally understood how Sarah couldn't make it. Of course she had to be there for her husband, but Jennifer would have preferred Sarah's company to anyone else here.

When Jennifer finished in the bathroom, she entered the restaurant and observed the table she was seated at was still waiting for mains. In the distance she heard a lot of excitement coming from the bar area, so decided to mosey on over and see what was happening.

The Zanzabar was jam-packed—no seats vacant

apart from one at the bar. Going out on a limb, Jennifer decided to take the seat at the bar. A young Asian man in his crisp white uniform served her a glass of house white. From where she was seated, she could see out into the foyer and noticed what looked to be a former student walk past the Zanzabar and into the Glasstop Restaurant. She knew the face, but couldn't remember his name.

Meredith Mason was seated at a table beside the bar. She saw Jennifer enter and take a seat at the bar and knew instantly she was way out of her comfort zone. She leaned over to Billy, her husband of twenty-two years, and said over the roar of the people watching the rugby world cup at the far end of the bar: "Check her out, she hasn't stepped foot in a bar in a long time. Totally out of her comfort zone, wouldn't you agree?"

Billy turned to see who his wife was referring to and instantly agreed with her: "Most definitely, sweetheart, you've hit the nail on the head."

One of the teams had just scored a goal. Meredith could see they were dressed in black and although she couldn't see the score but obviously the All Blacks were winning.

The Masons watched Jennifer for a while. They noticed she never turned around to look at the crowd in the bar. As Jennifer quietly sipped her glass of wine, Meredith walked over and asked if she would like to sit at their table. Jennifer thanked her, but declined the invitation. A little too quickly, Jennifer downed the drink and walked back into the restaurant. She glanced over to her table; thank god the mains had arrived, she was starving.

The table was relatively quiet as they ate. Jennifer,

who was seated with her back to the next table, was annoyed when the silence was broken with cheers of congratulations. She turned to look behind to see a large group of people make a champagne toast. Trying not to be nosey she couldn't help but hear what the toasts were for.

A young woman had accepted a job in Hong Kong and, a young man a job as an associate at a law firm in New York.

Jennifer was impressed; being a lecturer in law she knew only too well how hard it was to get a job as an associate. To be offered an associate position in New York was a real coup. Through the reflection in the window Jennifer couldn't see who it was, but she could tell this person was quite young. She wondered what his story was, where had he studied, to be offered such an incredible position. Then it occurred to her that maybe it was the student she had seen earlier. But that couldn't be, his grades were borderline, she remembered that much. His name would come to her, eventually.

After she had finished her meal, Jennifer accepted the conversation at the table was boring her; she grabbed her bag, said her goodbyes and headed to the Zanzabar. Billy and Meredith Mason were still there. As she walked into the bar, Meredith looked up and beckoned her over; this time, Jennifer accepted.

Drinks with the Masons were certainly more enjoyable than her meal earlier. Jennifer was surprised that the Masons had only been on the island a week, but seemed to know almost everyone. Meredith took great delight in pointing out people, revealing their personal stories, or what she had learned of them.

Meredith asked about her lunch conversation to which Jennifer mentioned she'd overheard that famous musician Lenni Maxwell lived on the island.

"Ah! Lenni Maxwell, he was in here the other night, met with a property developer Grant Woodham; we observed them having a heated discussion over dinner. Not that they ate anything. Lenni didn't stay long enough to be served; he stormed out before the waiter took their order. He was not very happy and then Grant stormed out of the restaurant after him, nearly knocking over one of the wait staff."

Meredith continued, "We weren't aware of who it was that Lenni had dinner with until the next day when we saw the mystery man out by the pool. We just happened to sit beside him and got talking about his visit to the island. He was pretty tight-lipped, but we found out he was a property developer. Although he wouldn't reveal what he was doing on the island, and no, we didn't mention we saw the confrontation between the two of them. It seemed pointless. He wasn't giving anything away, was he Billy?" Billy nodded his head in agreement.

CHAPTER SEVEN

Money Can Buy Anything

Lenni Maxwell had been singing professionally since he was eight years old, music was in his blood. His lifestyle was a direct reflection of how much money he had acquired.

His face told no lies—the years of living the high life; the long nights, alcohol, drug addiction and an unhealthy diet had taken its toll and he wasn't yet forty.

His body was showing the signs as well. He now relied on heavy makeup and long gone were the tight-fitting outfits he wore to stand out from the crowd. He didn't need to attract women anymore; there was always a constant supply of women on hand. No matter where he toured, he was always surrounded by young, desperate groupies who were willing to offer their bodies to him at any cost.

When Lenni first came to Clairemont Island it was to rest his voice after vocal nodules were removed surgically. His surgeon had recommended the island as a quiet getaway retreat. Resting his vocal cords for a week was the desired outcome, before undergoing vocal therapy before his next tour.

As Lenni recovered in one of the honeymoon suites, he would never forget the first time he laid eyes on Lucy. He was sitting on the balcony in just his boxer shorts, enjoying the warm afternoon sun. Lucy had knocked on his hotel room door.

"Housekeeping," she shouted to be heard over the music playing in the room. She waited a few minutes before knocking again. "Housekeeping, may I clean your room?"

She looked up from the clipboard she was holding and caught sight of a man who looked familiar, but she couldn't put her finger on how she might know him. Perhaps he's been a guest here before, she concluded.

"Hello sir, may I clean your room?" Lenni nodded and proceeded to let her into the suite. He made his way back onto the balcony, but didn't sit down immediately; he stood watching her. He was mesmerised by her youthful beauty. She was certainly a stunning girl, her olive complexion and curvy body with tight firm breasts were a sight for sore eyes, to say the least.

He decided to change his seat so he could watch her work. After she left he wrote a note to housekeeping, requesting that she should be the only person to clean his room while he was a guest at the resort. He personally delivered the note to the concierge on his way to dinner that night.

Lucy, unaware of the request he had made, was directed to the rooms to clean from the list attached to her clipboard. It was the second day she cleaned his room that he made advances on her. She was as horny as hell and didn't give it a second thought—and he tipped her generously.

When she first started meeting the needs of the guests she was shocked at how generously they tipped, but it all added to her escape fund, so she didn't care what it took.

By the end of that first week cleaning Lenni's room, she had made quite an impression on him. Their lovemaking was fast and furious during the day as she cleaned, but the invitation to join him at night after dinner was more adventurous—long and slow, and he did things to her no other man had done before. At times, she didn't like it, but the more he experimented with her, the more she was willing to let him do anything. By now, she knew who he was . . . her meal ticket out of here.

He bought his secluded mansion on Clairemont Island on that visit. He had not wanted to leave; he didn't want to give up Lucy, but he didn't want to ask her to join him either.

This mansion, his slice of heaven, as he called it, was bought with the intention to spend time there in between gigs, away from the paparazzi.

Over the last few years, he had managed to get away for just a few nights at a time, but his body was yearning for a much longer reboot.

Each time he headed towards the seclusion of the island it didn't take him long to miss the chaotic madness the entourage that hung around him night and day caused. In an effort to sustain some kind of normality, he always put the word out on the island that everyone was welcome to his house parties.

This weekend was no exception; it was an open

house, just the way Lenni liked it.

He never invited Lucy personally, but he knew she would come, she always did.

CHAPTER EIGHT

Observations

A month at home to recuperate from his heart attack was exactly what Dwayne needed—to search for work and to observe what was happening on the home front.

Was it his imagination or was his marriage really in ruins, and could it be saved? That was what he was going to assess over the next few weeks.

His specialist had booked his visits to the cardiac nurse and a physiotherapist as his rehabilitation program, but Dwayne had asked for a referral to a counsellor as well. He had come to realise, thanks to Sally, his sympathetic nurse, that he may be the cause of this marriage being in the state it was in. If he really wanted to make changes, he might first have to look within to find the answers.

Thankfully, he could say his visits to the counsellor were because of his heart attack and Susan wouldn't need to know about these confidential meetings—that is, if she even cared to ask.

Dwayne improved greatly, according to his physiotherapist, which was a weight off his shoulders. At home, he rested as much as he could, but more importantly he paid considerable attention to his wife. He was determined to identify what was going on there; if there was a glimmer of hope he was going to save his marriage.

Susan showed genuine concern for his welfare, always checking to see if he needed anything, which was a good sign. There had been no attempt to connect on a romantic level. He had tried to snuggle into her, but she pulled away from him, escaping to her own side of the bed. He lay there, pretending to sleep, feeling rejected, and wondered why she had pulled away. He used to embrace her until they fell asleep; the smell of her perfume lingering on her body, the delicate feel of her soft silky hair as he nestled into the nape of her neck. Yes, he remembered, but how long had it been since he last experienced this loving connection with his wife? He couldn't remember.

He was dubious about going to Lenni's party; it had been ages since he'd been out and years since he'd gone anywhere without Susan.

Kathy called in to check up on him Thursday afternoon, armed with gifts from Clairemont Supermarket. Denzel Woods, Mayor of Clairemont Island and owner of the supermarket, had organised a huge gift basket of local produce that his wife Sabrina had gathered up as she did her round of meetings and networking events. It was a small island and Dwayne was well respected, so people gave generously.

Deliberately timing her visit so that Dwayne would be home alone, Kathy was interested to hear what, if any, solutions he had come up with over the week. She found him sitting outside in the afternoon sun.

"So, tell me all about your week, what have you observed and what decisions have you made?" Kathy asked apprehensively.

"I definitely want to look for another job. I've scanned the local papers and there are quite a few on the mainland that I can apply for, although nothing here on the island. But in saying that, I think I'll approach some of the people I know who use mainland bookkeepers and ask if they'd consider taking me on if they know I'm available.

"I started to update my resume and realised it was so old I may as well start from scratch, after all I've been at the supermarket for almost fifteen years. Would you be able to give me a hand next week to create a new one?"

"Of course, I'll do anything to help." Kathy's look of devotion was all he needed to feel confident about the next step forward.

"How about Susan, any changes on that front?" Kathy asked cautiously, but then wished she hadn't as she saw tears well up in his eyes.

"I love her so much I can hardly contain myself, but to be honest I didn't realise things had gotten so bad. I don't know if it's entirely my fault or if we are both at fault for letting our marriage get to this stage.

"I've noticed heaps this last week, while I was in the Medical Centre and here at home.

He wanted to say-we don't seem to kiss anymore; I

Vicki Williams

can't remember the last time I made love to her or if she even enjoys it. I can't remember the last time she had an orgasm. I can't remember the last time we embraced each other romantically, but he was too ashamed and embarrassed to mention how he felt and that she had pulled away from him the night before.

"We're civil to each other and ask how each other's day has been, but the art of conversation seems to be lacking. It's as if we don't care about each other anymore and I reckon it's from both sides.

"It's breaking my heart. I'm not sure how to change it, but I know I want to. Or rather, I have to change, because now I know just how bad it has become I can't live like this any longer.

"I've already decided that tonight when she comes home I'm going to ask her if she is happy with our marriage and, from that, figure out how we can fix it. I have to give it everything I've got."

After Kathy left, Dwayne wrote a list of questions he wanted to ask Susan.

Emily didn't disappoint; she came home from school, disappeared into her room for a couple of hours and then announced she was going to a friend's place to study for an exam. Emily and Susan passed each other at the front door.

Dwayne poured Susan a glass of wine as he set the table for dinner, four hours later, after an honest and open discussion about their life, marriage and individual aspirations, the conversation ended on a positive note.

He had the answers to his questions and was satisfied with the responses and for the first time in ages, he felt content and more optimistic about his future.

Both Susan and Dwayne admitted they weren't happy about the condition of their marriage and promised they would work at re-connecting with each other and re-establish a relationship with Emily while she was still living at home.

"I appreciate you cooking dinner tonight, but please don't expect me home for dinner any night this week, I've got so much on, I'll be lucky to make it home before midnight." Susan wanted to prepare him for her absence this week, she didn't want him to worry unnecessarily.

"I'm really pleased that business is booming, but why don't I cook dinner and bring it to you at the office, you have to eat and that way we will get to spend some time together." Dwayne offered.

"You can't drive, and to be honest I'll be working right through. I'm in the middle of a massive property development and the paperwork is driving me insane. That pile of papers over there doesn't even scratch the surface." Susan gestured to the paperwork she'd bought home to work on that night.

Knowing Susan was going to be working on Saturday night, he decided not to mention that he might go out, that way he wouldn't have to lie to her.

On Saturday afternoon, Kathy called to see if he had decided about going to the party. He felt OK within himself, he wasn't tired after his exercise that morning; in fact, each day he was feeling more energetic.

"Why not, Susan is working late, she's been burning the candle at both ends, so even if she did come home from work early, chances are she'd crash, she's exhausted."

"Ok, Simon and I will pick you up at 8:00 p.m."

CHAPTER NINE

Open Arms

Lucy met Troy at 8:00 p.m. in the car park of the Clairemont Resort; the party was on the other side of the island and a little hard to find if you were attending for the first time. Lucy was a regular at these parties. There was a handful of regulars who always attended. They waited in anticipation for Lenni to come to the island, to resource them with a never-ending supply of booze and drugs.

As Troy entered Lenni's home, he noticed couples scattered in the many lounges, drinking and shouting over the loud music playing throughout the house via a sound system. The entertainment area located at the rear of the property was where Lenni hung out and that was where Lucy was leading Troy.

Troy knew only too well what the group of people was doing over the kitchen bench. Cocaine was his drug of choice, but he was open to any drug on offer. This was part of his life now, had been for many years—he was thrilled to see that tonight he would get a fix. He wasn't sure what Lucy's reaction would be; he didn't know if she partook or not. Hopefully, he would meet the host, get the pleasantries out of the way then excuse himself before making his way to the kitchen to join the crowd openly enjoying the sweet taste of gold dust.

It wasn't hard to figure out who the host was, he was the short stocky balding guy surrounded by youthful skimpily-clad women, hanging on his every word, or what they could hear, over the annoyingly loud music. Troy stood back, waiting for Lucy to make her way through the group of young beauties. When the host turned around to greet Lucy, Troy realised this was Lenni Maxwell. Troy loved his music; he wondered why Lucy didn't mention it was Lenni's party.

As Lucy went to introduce Troy to Lenni, Lenni grabbed his hand and led him away to the other side of the pool, gesturing Troy to sit at a table setting under a large umbrella.

"Troy, it's been years, how the hell are you mate?" Lenni said as he frantically shook Troy's hand. "What would you like to drink?" asked Lenni.

Troy looked around the crowd to see what was on offer: "Beer, thanks."

"Lucy, grab us some beers, love," Lenni shouted across the pool to Lucy, who was talking to one of her friends.

"Troy, welcome to my home, it's a far cry from our uni days together, but you are welcome here anytime. If there is anything you want, anything, he gestured with open arms; women, booze or any drug of choice, it's all here just help yourself, OK?"

"OK, thanks, Lenni, I appreciate the offer," Troy

thanked Lenni. In a way Lenni would never understand, tonight was going to be an incredible night; Troy couldn't believe his luck.

At that moment, Lucy handed each of them a can of beer and asked how they knew each other.

Lenni was the first to reply.

"Troy and I both attended university together, albeit it was only for a year. My parents were adamant that I get some kind of qualification. I wasn't academic and to be honest my only passion was singing, but back then my parents didn't think that was enough. My father, a lawyer thought I would make a good lawyer, I've no idea why, it didn't interest me. But to keep them happy I enrolled and the first thing I did was start a band and we played nearly every night. That's how I met Troy, he was a regular, a real ladies man if memory serves correctly. To cut a long story short, I didn't do any study and was soon asked to leave. By then my parents had succumbed to the fact music was in my blood, and they agreed that I may actually be good enough to make money from it, which I clearly did."

They enjoying each other's company, talking about the good old days eventually, Troy excused himself to visit the bathroom. On the way he checked the situation in the kitchen; noticing a cupboard full of coke he knew there was no rush, they weren't going to run out tonight.

He took his time finding the bathroom. Checking out what the huddled groups were partaking in, he realised this was indeed going to be a great night.

The front door was wide open and clusters of people in different rooms were doing all kinds of drugs. He saw pills lying all over the place, pills of every colour imaginable, uppers, downers—you name it, it was here. In his effort to find the bathroom he observed people on couches, on the floor, one couple looked to be totally out of it standing up against the wall.

The bathroom had seen its fair share of use, not your typical standard of cleanliness for this opulent room. Half empty wine glasses and beer bottles were strewn all over the vanity and on the floor by the toilet that showed tell-tale signs of people having had too much of a good time. One young girl was passed out in the bath; vomit streaked down the front of her short skimpy tee shirt, her skirt was up around her waist, revealing what could only be described as a pencil thin thong.

Troy urinated, not really caring how accurate his aim was, apparently nobody else had either. As he walked out of the bathroom, he gazed out the window to see Lucy straddling Lenni's lap, gyrating in a familiar rhythm. It took him by surprise that she would openly have sex with Lenni. Having made such a big deal to invite him along tonight, Troy had automatically expected to be taking her home, but hey; maybe this is how it's done on the island.

Making a bee-line for the kitchen, the hunger to feed his addiction had become more important than heading back outside. If he was right and Lucy was making love to Lenni, then it looked like he was going home alone, so he may as well enjoy what was on offer—he'd be a fool not to. He took his time cutting the coke and as every snort hit home, he thanked god for the pleasures of the sins he'd experienced over the last few days.

Normally, like everyone else in the house, he

would spend some time in his own thoughts, enjoying the buzz and trying desperately not to think about how cocked up his life was, but tonight he couldn't relax—something was niggling at him and he didn't know what it was.

The music was blaring loudly, he couldn't hear himself think. If he could find the control he would turn it down, even just a little would make a huge difference.

He set off to find the control, gazing around each of the two oversized lounge rooms that surrounded the kitchen; they were elegant and tastefully furnished: each room was set out the same, consisting of three large comfortable white couches arranged in a U shape with a glass topped mahogany coffee table in the middle of them. Smaller identical side tables were placed at the ends of each of the couches, table lamps sat on the tables in the two corners, containing the area and creating a comfortable, inviting feeling.

A massive 175 cm. TV hung on the wall, perfectly positioned for all to see. The rest of the room was dressed with mahogany cabinets full of trinkets Lenni had collected on his travels. Artwork hanging precariously around the walls seemed out of place, the tone and texture didn't seem to go with the rest of the ambience. Most pieces were dangling at unusual angles and seemed to have been tampered with, as if someone had gone in search of a safe.

Still in search of the sound system control, as the music was giving him one hell of a headache, he started trying the doors to the rooms that were previously open; gently he tried a door handle to see if it was locked before quietly opening it. Most rooms now revealed a number of bodies in different stages of undress; all were passed out except one young woman. She was frantically trying to find her clothes as Troy entered the room. Startled by him, she automatically held her arms around her body to shield herself from his gaze.

"Can you help me find my clothes?" she asked.

"Do you want me to turn the light on?" Troy asked.

"No, I don't want to wake anyone," she whispered as she gazed over to the group of bodies on the bed. "But I do have to get home before my curfew."

Curfew! Oh my God thought Troy, what age was this girl? Shuddering to think, he helped her by holding up an array of clothing, eventually finding her excuse for a dress, she quickly pulled it down over her braless breasts and thong.

What on earth do these girls think when they dress like this, what's their intention? he wondered. But in saying that, he knew; he was always drawn to the ones that showed their body through their clothes, the long-legged beauties that revealed almost everything when they moved. Yes, he thought to himself, they know exactly what they are doing. Sex sells and he is always tempted to buy.

Troy walked around the corner that led to even more rooms. He hadn't seen this end of the house when he entered from the front door only hours earlier. One door was open and he recognised it immediately as the office—the large mahogany desk took pride of place and dominated the room. The oversized leather chair complemented it perfectly.

To both sides of the desk were filing cabinets and more chairs, only smaller. Troy noticed the artwork in this room was more tasteful, hung evenly, with precision. He identified it was probably installed when the rest of the house was furnished: the room felt complete.

Just two more doors to open, both were closed; he tried the door on his left and it opened quietly to reveal the master bedroom. Nobody was in the room; obviously, they knew it was out of bounds. Neat and tidy, this room was decorated in soft gold tones, fitting he thought for someone with a vast fortune.

Wall to wall glass lined most of the room; on closer inspection he realised they were cupboards and having no handles made the room look more impressive. He touched the corner in a couple of places and they opened to reveal loads of hidden personal belongings.

The ensuite was immaculate, nothing like the state of the bathroom he'd been in earlier; clearly this bathroom hadn't been used today. Realising the sound system was not in the master bedroom he headed to the last door, his head still pounding.

The coke he'd snorted in the kitchen earlier had not given him the outcome he'd desired. He couldn't imagine Lenni would have been sold an inferior batch of cocaine. Most people who had partaken in the pleasure were off their faces, so it must be him, maybe he needed more coke. He decided to cruise by the kitchen again after checking out this last room.

As he went to open this last door, he noticed it slightly ajar; pushing it open fully, Troy walked into the music studio. He noticed immediately a control panel in front of the glass booth, where Lenni clearly recorded his music tracks. The control panel was completely foreign to him, but after sliding some buttons up and down he noticed a difference in sound, somewhat distorted, but most definitely a lot quieter.

Satisfied with his accomplishment, he turned to leave. As he did so he noticed behind the control panel was a lounge area with chairs and a coffee table. His vision fixed immediately on the bag of cocaine sitting on the table; beside it was a glass tray with some unused lines.

Troy was just about to help himself when he heard Lucy yelling out for him. Feeling somewhat disappointed with the timing, he walked quickly to the door; closing it behind him, he made his way to Lucy who was helping herself to a glass a water in the kitchen. The tray of cocaine was no longer sitting on the bench.

"I've got a splitting headache," Lucy said. "Do you want to split?" Nodding in agreement, Troy told her his head was pounding as well. Walking toward the front door, which was still wide open, Troy noticed some of the occupants had moved on.

The clock in Lucy's car showed 11:30 p.m. Troy was surprised; it didn't feel like they had been at Lenni's that long. Maybe time does fly when you're having fun, he thought. He didn't mention what he thought he'd seen happen between Lenni and Lucy. She wasn't very talkative, not like on the way there, when he could hardly shut her up. Maybe she does have a headache, he thought; his head was certainly throbbing.

As Lucy parked the car at the resort car park, she looked over to Troy and asked quietly: "Would you like company or would you like to be alone, because I'm as horny as hell?" He looked at her like a stunned mullet, then nodded in agreement. If she was horny then maybe she didn't bang Lenni earlier this evening.

His mood changed instantly. "Of course I'd love to," he replied, without giving it a second thought.

Their lovemaking that night was different, more intimate and he wondered if it was because they actually talked. She asked him about his life, his problems, his dreams, his desires and he felt relieved to get it off his chest.

Troy asked Lucy about her life on the island and for once she was honest about herself. She shared some stories about her childhood, and in doing so the memories brought her to tears. Troy didn't speak; he had no idea what to say to comfort her, so instead he held her tightly until they fell asleep.

He woke at 2:00 a.m. tossing and turning, he looked around, but unfortunately she'd gone. He lay there, unable to go back to sleep, reflecting on what she'd shared, then desperately wondered how he was going to fix his own dilemma. On the surface, his life looked fantastic, but in reality, it had taken a turn for the worse and this time he felt ill equipped to fix it.

CHAPTER TEN

Betrayal

When Dwayne, Kathy and Simon arrived at Lenni's house the front door was wide open, music blaring and people everywhere. It felt as if the whole island was here at the party. Dwayne asked if this was normal. Simon shrugged his shoulders and announced he didn't know—he'd never been to a party here before.

Simon grabbed a beer and handed one to Kathy, in doing so he noticed Dwayne grab an orange juice as they started mingling. Dwayne knew a lot of people at the party from his role as football coach. He talked to most of them and was surprised at the openness of the young people partaking in drugs— well, it certainly looked like they were doing drugs. He was in no way an expert; he had never used drugs, he didn't know anything about them. His drug of choice was beer.

As he watched from afar he wondered if his football team did drugs during the football season.

Admittedly they weren't in a league that warranted a squeaky-clean record, but he wondered if some of the very talented guys used any illegal substances during the football season. A few of those boys were here tonight enjoying themselves. If I do coach next year, I may just look into this further.

Kathy walked over to re-join Simon and Dwayne after spending some time catching up with old friends. What she'd just learned was something she wished she had never been told. Escaping outside for some fresh air and a chance to digest the shocking news, she felt she couldn't win regardless of what she did, so being the bigger person she decided to come right out and say it.

With a glass of wine and a couple of beers for the men, she motioned they all sit down at a table setting away from everyone else.

"No thanks, Kathy, I can't drink this soon after my heart attack," Dwayne replied. Kathy didn't pull back, instead she literally thrust the can of beer into his hand.

"Trust me, Dwayne, with what I have to tell you, you will need the beer," Kathy asserted.

Simon looked apprehensively at Kathy. "What's going on, what's happened?" It was getting quite noisy outside, but Kathy huddled forward and both Simon and Dwayne followed suit.

"I was just talking to Zara and Adam, they asked how you were after your heart attack and I said you were making great progress. They asked if your finding out about Susan caused your heart attack. I had no idea what they were talking about. The sad thing was they thought everyone knew. Then they told me that Susan is having an affair with Lenni.

Seems to have been going on for ages.

I didn't know anything about it, did you?" Kathy looked questioningly at Dwayne, but she could tell immediately he hadn't known either.

"No, that can't be possible," Dwayne responded in an attempt to defend his wife's honour.

"I'm sorry, Dwayne, but Adam is Lenni's gardener and Adam said he has seen Susan here many times. He even has a photo of them in Lenni's bedroom. He caught them in the act, as it seems they forgot to pull the curtains. He showed me the photo and it's definitely Susan.

"I'm sorry to have to tell you this, but maybe it's all come at the right time; this may be what you have unconsciously been thinking is wrong with your marriage. Maybe you suspected all along and that's why you two have become so distant."

Simon took one look at his defeated friend and suggested they leave. "This is probably the last place you want to be right now, and I don't want you to do anything silly and cause another heart attack, so come on, let's get out of here."

Dwayne snapped a little too quickly: "You know what pisses me off the most, we talked for hours the other night and we both agreed that we needed to work on our marriage, and all the time she was lying to me, lying to my face, the bitch. All this time she's been unfaithful, and I thought I was doing something wrong. Thanks mate, but I'm not going anywhere yet. I'm here at a party and I'm going to enjoy myself, so come on, let's grab another beer and start living. I'll deal with her later.

"She's not expecting me to be here. Wouldn't it be funny if she turned up, then I can have it out with her once and for all. Quite fitting isn't it? And if it causes another heart attack, it may just kill me this time and that would solve all our problems."

Kathy and Simon sat in stunned silence as Dwayne walked off into the crowd. In the distance, Kathy could see Lenni surrounded by gorgeous young girls hanging off his every word. Yes, Susan was beautiful, but Kathy struggled to think Susan was in Lenni's league. She just didn't seem the type somehow, but then what would she know about Lenni's type.

Sipping her glass of wine, she kept a close eye on Lenni, just in case Dwayne confronted him about the alleged affair with his wife.

Simon had followed Dwayne to make sure he didn't do anything stupid like attack Lenni. Dwayne had stopped to talk to the twins, Faye and Faith. He wasn't sure what medication Dwayne was on for his heart attack, but it didn't take a rocket scientist to know that medication and alcohol weren't a good mix.

Dwayne was now onto his fourth can of beer and getting way too familiar with the twins: they seemed to be flattered by his over-friendly advances. He wasn't too sure what he should do when Dwayne led the twins into one of the rooms down the hall.

Making his way back to his wife, Simon told Kathy what he had observed, admitting he didn't know what to do. Should he have stopped him?

"Think about it, he's just had a massive blow. The heart attack, identifying he isn't happy in his marriage, and then finding out his wife has been having an affair. Hell, that's pretty massive, don't you think?"

"Yeah, you're right, but can he have sex after a heart attack? He's had four cans of beer, I don't know what medication he's on, but that's a lot, isn't it?" Simon looked at his wife wanting some reassurance that they hadn't just made things worse.

"I suppose when you think about it, he's trying to prove to himself that he still has what it takes to make love to a woman. Seems his wife hasn't been interested in him and now we know why. He probably just wants to know there's nothing wrong with him and he's still attracted to the opposite sex."

"I'm just pleased he didn't attack Lenni. I certainly didn't think that through when I announced the bombshell here at this house. To take two gorgeous young girls into a bedroom means nothing, and to be honest, who cares if he does or doesn't make love to them? It's none of our business. Let's just hang around and make sure he doesn't get himself into any trouble."

Kathy sat so she could see the hallway that led to the bedroom where Dwayne had taken the twins. From where she sat she also had an uninterrupted view of Lenni out by the pool; she wanted to keep an eye on him, just in case Susan turned up. Who knows what would erupt if that happened.

Almost an hour later Dwayne emerged from the bedroom looking a little flushed, but somewhat proud of himself. The twins were nowhere to be seen. He quietly made his way over to Kathy and Simon and announced he was ready to head home.

Nothing was said on the way back to Dwayne's house. It was none of their business and Dwayne wasn't saying anything.

Susan's car was not in the driveway as they pulled

up to the house. Kathy wondered if it was safe to leave him alone especially after having all those beers. Dwayne reassured them he was OK, so they settled him into bed and left him to mull over what had eventuated that night.

As he lay in bed, Dwayne couldn't get the thought of Susan and Lenni out of his head. How could she sit across the table from him and swear black and blue that she would work on their relationship—he felt like a fool, how gullible was he?

At midnight Susan still hadn't arrived home and he wondered if she was at the party. Let's be honest, where else could she possibly be? Her mobile was turned off; he'd tried to call her about ten times since he arrived home. All he could do was sink deeper into depression as he waited and waited for his wife to return home. His car was parked in the driveway; he could drive up there and find out for himself if that's where she was. Have it out with both of them. What else could he do now that he knew?

He knew his doctor had forbidden him to drive, but this was a matter of urgency. If he didn't find out where she was, this betrayal would slowly kill him anyway.

At 1:00 a.m. he made a decision. He knew this decision would allow him to move forward with his life—he also knew there would be no turning back from it.

CHAPTER ELEVEN

One Hell Of A Party

"Doctor Scott here Gabby, I've got some bad news and wonder if you can do me a favour and send over James, your head of security, and if Ramon, your photographer is available. I reckon we'll need his services as well."

"Sure thing, Scotty, but what's happened", asked Gabby Saintclaire, manager of Clairemont Resort.

"Ella Martin, one of your cleaners went to clean Lenni Maxwell's home this morning only to find him dead, floating face down in his pool. She called me because she didn't know who else to call, seeing as there's no police on the island.

"When I arrived, I couldn't believe the state of the house; seems he'd had one hell of a party. Not sure at this stage what killed him, probably a drug overdose, knowing his lifestyle. An autopsy and toxicology report will confirm if it was drugs or something else. From where I'm standing, I can see dried blood on the back of his head, but I can't see any other visible signs. I won't know more until I examine his body. I wanted to get your photographer over to take photos before I lug him out of the pool."

Oh my god, Lenni dead. I can only imagine the media frenzy and the paparazzi traipsing all over the island, it'll be a nightmare, Gabby reflected.

"No problems, Scotty, I'll get onto it right away, I'll bring James and Ramon to Lenni's house immediately, and I won't say a word to anyone. Obviously we don't want this to get out; has Ella mentioned it to anyone?" asked Gabby.

"No, I asked her to keep it quiet; she's too shaken to do anything at the moment. I've given her a sedative to calm her down, so I'm pleased you're coming over, you can help me keep an eye on her."

"Consider me on the way, see you soon."

The resort's security room wasn't an overly large room, but big enough to house the computers that monitored over fifty cameras strategically placed around the resort. There were five security guards that worked at the resort; James had been an employee for fifteen years. He was promoted to security manager five years ago.

James did not work weekends, so she called him on his mobile, "Good morning ma'am, how may I help you?"

"Morning. James. I'm sorry to bother you on a Sunday morning, but there's been a death on the island and we could certainly use your help. I'm on my way there now, are you able to join me?"

"Of course, Ms. Saintclaire. I'd be only too happy to help in any way I can. Can you pick me up at my home in ten minutes?"

Gabby then dialed Ramon, the resort

photographer, he lived in the resort, and it was a small price to pay for a photographer that was on call 24/7. He answered on the second ring.

"Good morning, Ramon speaking."

"Ramon, it's Gabby here. I'm wondering if you have anything on this morning. I could certainly use your help with something sensitive."

"I'm available all day Ms. Saintclaire, how can I help?"

"I'll explain on the way, can you also bring your underwater camera, we may need that. Could you meet me in the foyer in five minutes?"

"Certainly, see you then," replied Ramon.

At that moment, Gabby's husband, Michael, walked into her office. "What's on your agenda for the day, I was thinking we could get in a round of golf before the weather turns nasty, if you're interested?"

"Sorry, but I can't, Lenni Maxwell is dead. Ella found him this morning when she went to clean his house. Scotty called me just now to take James and Ramon over to his house.

"Anyway, must go, I'm not sure what time I'll be back, but you go golfing. When I was in the Zanzabar yesterday Andrew said he had today off, so he may want to get in a round of golf. Give him a call."

"Will do, see you later," whispered Michael as he kissed his wife goodbye.

True to his word, Ramon was in the foyer with his camera equipment when Gabby walked through from her office. "You have heard we are in for a cyclone, Ms. Saintclaire? What exactly would you like to photograph?" He had assumed it was a photo shoot for the resort, but wondered why he hadn't been part of the advisory team like he normally was.

As Gabby walked to the resort car that the managers used to get around the island, she glanced around to make sure nobody was in earshot. "Ramon, I'm going to pick up James, then I will explain everything, is that OK?"

"Certainly, Ms. Saintclaire, sounds pretty ominous, though," replied Ramon.

James lived a block away from the resort, in fact, he could have walked to the resort quicker than Gabby could drive to his house. His house backed onto the tennis court car park and he used that as a direct route to the resort.

James was waiting outside his modest home, the home he lived in with his wife and two children. Ramon jumped out of the passenger seat to offer it to James. Once James and Ramon had buckled themselves in, Gabby started off on their short journey to Lenni Maxwell's home.

"I must apologise for taking up your Sunday, but unfortunately, Lenni Maxwell was found dead this morning and Dr. Scott has asked for your help. As you know, we are in for a cyclone, so we need to make sure we take as many photos as possible of the house and crime scene without disturbing anything.

"Scotty said he hadn't touched the body; he wanted to wait until all the photos were taken. That's why I asked you to bring your underwater camera; apparently Lenni is face down in the pool. Let's get some photos of him from that angle. I'm not sure when mainland police can get over, so it's up to us to get what they want and secure the crime scene until they get here. James, you may need to call in some of your mates to help out with security of the property, but we can do that later."

Just then, Gabby pulled up outside Lenni's mansion. It was an impressive sight, relatively secluded up a winding path of conifers. From what Gabby had heard, Lenni had paid a fortune for it. She couldn't wait to see if the inside was just as impressive as the front of the property. Rumour had it, that the massive balcony from the master bedroom had breathtaking views of Clairemont Island, whereas the entertainment area overlooked its own secluded and private beach.

Scotty came to greet them as they got out of the car. "Thanks for coming. I didn't know who else to call. I haven't touched the body. I wanted to wait for you to take photos, Ramon.

Once you're finished with that I'll get you to help me get him out of the pool and then I can start my work.

Gabby, I have left Ella in the kitchen; she has just made a fresh pot of coffee."

"Can I interest any of you in something to drink," Gabby asked?

"No, thanks," they all answered in unison.

Scotty walked them through the house out to the pool. They noticed Ella sitting at the kitchen table still sobbing, her face showing the signs of a young woman in shock. Gabby walked over to Ella, sat down next to her and cradled her in her arms. Ella started sobbing all over again. Handing her a tissue, Gabby sat there and held her until she stopped crying.

"Ella, is it OK if I go outside and see if I can help Dr. Scott? I will only be a few moments and then I'll come back in, is that OK?" Ella nodded her head and Gabby rose from the table.

All around the pool area were wine glasses, beer bottles and ashtrays full of cigarettes and marijuana stubs. It was no better inside as Gabby noticed on the way through the house.

As Gabby, Scotty and James stood watching Ramon work, Scotty shared his first impression, although it was hard not to let assumptions get in the way.

It was a well-known fact that Lenni liked to party, and the state of his house was evidence of that. He had the reputation of being a ladies' man and, if what the papers said was correct, he also used drugs regularly.

Ramon motioned to them that he had finished photographing the body by pushing it to the side of the pool so James and Scotty could fish him out.

As Ramon dried himself and changed back into his clothes Scotty examined the body, Ramon and James started working inside the house, each room at a time. Ramon took photos of the room, taking in all the discarded bottles, and lipstick stains on glasses, and he photographed anything lying on the floor.

Just as they were about to leave the first room, Gabby noticed the artwork that was precariously hanging at unusual angles, it looked out of place and she asked Ramon if he had captured that on camera. He had, but admitted that he hadn't taken a close up of each one; they all agreed it seemed odd.

Leaving the boys to it, Gabby walked back to the kitchen to sit with Ella, who by this time had composed herself, eagerly accepting another cup of coffee. Gabby asked her to explain what had happened from the moment she arrived at the house earlier that morning.

"I was here last night; admittedly I had one too many drinks, so I slept in. The front door was wide open, which was unusual, so I looked around outside the front for Lenni, but didn't notice him. So I entered the house, yelling out that I was here, as I always did. I made my way to the cleaning cupboard and noticed Lenni's bedroom door open. I yelled out again, but he didn't respond so I looked into his room, noticing his bed was made. I thought that was weird, as he never makes his own bed.

"Music was blaring, which is nothing unusual, and I wondered if that was why he hadn't responded, so I walked around the house to find him. I always ask him which part of the house he wants cleaned first.

"I couldn't find him anywhere, so I went outside thinking he may be taking a swim, but he didn't usually do that after a party. He was usually hung over, and he was drinking when I left last night. I still couldn't find him, so I walked over to the edge of the pool area, where you get a good view of the beach, wondering if maybe he was down on the sand. Then I saw him in the pool. I didn't know what to do, so I called Dr. Scott.

"I was still standing at the pool when Dr. Scott arrived. I couldn't move—I've never seen a dead body before." After a moment of silence Ella quietly asked: "Why did Lenni have to die? He was really nice to me and gave me a job to help out since my dad's been out of work. Things are pretty tough at home."

Scotty came into the kitchen and asked for coffee. He waited until James and Ramon had finished, so they could help him load Lenni's body into his van to take back to the Medical Centre.

"I can't be certain yet, but I don't think he died of natural causes. It looks like blunt force trauma to the back of his head. He has bruising around his neck and the tops of his shoulders are scratched. If I'm not mistaken it looks to me like fingernail scratches. It may or may not be related, but I wonder if he had a fight with a woman last night?"

"Ella, you said you were here last night, can you remember who else was here and do you know if he had an argument or fight with anyone?" Scotty asked Ella as they sipped their coffee.

Gabby grabbed a notepad from her purse and started writing down the names as Ella recalled them.

"I was here with my boyfriend, Tim. Most of Tim's friends were here: Anton, Mitchell and Zara, Stella, Rosemary, Brenton, Darcy, Steve, Molly, June, Billy B, Billy Rune, and the twins, Faith and Fay.

"Mr. and Mrs. O'Connor left early. Mr. Olsen the football coach was here; the dirty old bugger was making a play for the twins. I'm sure there were more people here, but I can't think of them at the moment; if I think of anyone else I'll let you know."

"Was there anyone here that you didn't know?" asked Gabby.

"Yes. Lucy brought some hunky guy, not sure who he was. They were outside with Lenni for ages, talking business, I guess."

Gabby motioned Scotty to follow her; out of earshot, she asked Scotty if he had seen any evidence of drugs at the house when he arrived, because on the surface there were no signs of any.

Scotty admitted he hadn't looked around, but when Ella went to make coffee he noticed the tell-tale sign of cocaine residue on the kitchen bench.

"If that's the case, would you join me and James in searching the house to see if we can uncover anything here that may be related to his death?"

"Sure thing. Where should we start?" Scotty asked.

"Let's start from the front door and work our way to the outdoor area where Lenni was found," Gabby suggested.

Gabby, James and Scotty stood at the doorway of each of the rooms; carefully taking a mental picture of everything in the room, just as Ramon had done with his camera. Only Gabby was looking for what was out of place like with the artwork in the front lounge. She was trying to piece together what, if anything, could be missing, even though she had never set foot in the house before.

Gabby was pleased that Scotty had an analytical mind. It helped to bounce ideas off him. She was a Virgo, a perfectionist—neat, tidy and everything in its place.

She didn't know what star sign Lenni was, but she could tell from the layout of the rooms that either he or his housekeeper was a perfectionist, as everything was symmetrically placed and perfectly positioned, making it easy to see if something was missing or out of place. Admittedly, some trinkets had been pushed out of the way by partygoers.

"Ella, are you Lenni's only cleaner?"

"Yes. Mrs. Olsen, who sold Lenni the house, is a really good friend of my Mum, so when he asked for a cleaner she recommended me."

"When did you last clean the house?" Gabby asked.

"I came in on Wednesday because Lenni was due to arrive on Thursday; apart from that, I was here last night."

"Can you see anything that is out of place or missing?" Scotty asked Ella. "Walk with us and let us know if you see anything unusual."

In the master bedroom, she mentioned again that Lenni never made his own bed. This meant he hadn't slept in it since arriving on the island on Thursday. Gabby asked if that was unusual.

"Yes, but sometimes beds in the other rooms need to be changed. I've no idea who sleeps in them, and it's none of my business," Ella stated. It was something that she had questioned, but never had the nerve to ask, knowing it would overstep the bound of friendship.

The music studio was in a hell of a mess. Gabby's immediate thought was that it had been ransacked. Ella said that sometimes when she came to clean she wasn't allowed in the music studio, especially if Lenni was busy working, and when she eventually did get in to clean, it looked like this, a hell of a mess.

James had turned off the music that had been playing since they arrived. There was an airy feel to the room as if it had a life of its own, and with the music turned off, the quietness of the room was almost deafening.

When they got to the office, Gabby wondered if he had a current will, or at least contact details of someone they should call. James carefully made his way through the filing cabinets and desk drawers, but didn't find anything of importance; perhaps Lenni kept those sensitive documents at one of his other houses.

Gabby asked Scotty if he had seen a mobile phone on Lenni, as she hadn't noticed one lying around the house. Scotty hadn't seen one on his body, and nobody had noticed a mobile outside. Funny, they thought, where was it, perhaps someone had taken it by mistake?

Congregating back in the kitchen, one of James's colleagues had arrived to do the first shift of guarding the property.

James had called through to the mainland police and spoken to Detective Inspector Katrina Reid. He explained everything they had done.

She was pleased to hear that they had used common sense and taken photos before entering any of the rooms, James explained he had posted a team of security personnel to ensure the property remained contained until her team arrived as soon as possible after the cyclone. Gabby had never worked with Katrina, but she knew of her by reputation and held a lot of respect for her. She knew they would be in good hands when she eventually arrived on the island.

It was agreed they had no option but to clear up all the debris left behind from the party. They packed away the outdoor furniture into the storage areas adjacent to the house, making sure they securely locked up the property in preparation for the impending cyclone.

CHAPTER TWELVE

Deception

Arriving back at the resort, Gabby thanked both James and Ramon. She asked for discretion, as she wanted the issue contained for as long as possible.

Gabby didn't go back to her office; instead she headed to their apartment, as she felt the need of a shower and a stiff drink. Grateful that Michael was not there, she needed the time alone to think about what she had just witnessed.

On returning from the golf course, Michael opened the door to their apartment just as Gabby poured a steaming hot coffee.

"Tell me all about what happened with you today," Michael asked as he sat down at the kitchen table with his wife.

Gabby relayed everything that had happened.

"Seems like all of you were the perfect team. Let's hope D.I. Reid can figure out what happened to Lenni quickly so that we can keep the paparazzi to a minimum. The island will be destroyed with them traipsing all over it," Michael acknowledged.

"Yeah, I've been thinking about that and wanted to get your advice on something," said Gabby.

"What's troubling you, love?" Michael hesitantly responded.

"We both know as soon as this gets out the paparazzi are going to be all over the island. What if we said the island was fully booked out, maybe they wouldn't come?"

Michael attempted to reassure her: "I totally agree with you, love, but we are in the hospitality business, or had you forgotten? Let's be honest, keeping our occupancy rate up is our biggest challenge, and what would Roger say if we lied about our occupancy rate? Lost revenue is not what he is paying us for.

"As much as I agree with you, we'd be in a pack of trouble if we followed through, but there's no stopping us talking to Roger about it. We probably need to speak to him about Lenni's death anyway, considering a lot of our staff were at his party and could potentially be connected. We'd better check in and see how he wants us to handle the media frenzy."

Self-made property tycoon, Roger Jackson, had owned Clairemont Resort for twenty-five years; he had employed Gabby and Michael to manage it so that he could open a similar style of resort in Hawaii.

Michael made the call to Roger; he explained what had happened to Lenni and their concern about what the paparazzi could do to the eco-footprint of the island and the reputation of the resort.

Michael was not a fan of the media and he knew

Roger felt the same way, so he was interested to hear what Roger had to say about their predicament.

Five years ago, just as Michael and Gabby took over as hotel managers, the resort went down with food poisoning. As a result, they copped some pretty bad press.

A few mainland TV stations hit the island like a tornado and, with only half the correct information, went about laying blame in all the wrong places. As a result, many local businesses were severely affected. When the truth finally came out it was too late; the bad press had killed the tourist industry on the island for many years.

Of course, the circumstances were different this time around, but the press had a habit of dredging up the past—they would do anything to get news, and they didn't care who they hurt along the way.

"Michael, I understand where you're coming from and I do sympathise with you, but unfortunately business is business and it's just not practical to turn a guest away, regardless of who they are. You understand, don't you?"

"Yes, I do, unfortunately," Michael responded, feeling somewhat disheartened.

Just as Michael was about to hang up, Roger suddenly remembered a conversation he'd had a few weeks back, that had totally slipped his mind until now.

"Michael, I had a call from a property developer, his name was Grant Woodham.

"He said Coastal Developments was building condos on the island with Lenni Maxwell and wondered what I was doing with the land I owned adjacent to the resort, or if I was in a position to sell it. When I said I had no intention of selling, he then asked if I had any connections on the council. Seems he wants to tie up some loose ends and wanted a connection through the back door.

"I didn't think any more about it until now, but, if he is tying up loose ends, this says to me that it's the end of the process, not the start. Chances are, he wasn't interested in my land at all, but the call was really about getting a council connection.

"Have you heard anything about condos being built on the island, or any land that's been sold off?" Roger asked Michael.

"No, I haven't. I can ask Gabby, but I'm not aware of anything major happening on the island and something like that would get around pretty fast.

"Roger, everything is done on the mainland. We only have a skeleton crew of council workers here on the island, so my thoughts are that he wanted to know who to get into bed with here to get applications and approvals done under the radar," Michael said.

"With Lenni dead, I wonder where that leaves the project, especially if he was one of the developers. Interesting to see what stage this is at, but I'm sure the media will fill us all in if Lenni had anything to do with it," Michael agreed with Roger. As they said their goodbyes they were both deep in thought.

CHAPTER THIRTEEN

A Star Is Born

"Ms. Saintclaire, it's Ella here. I just remembered Lenni has a personal assistant. Her name is Simone Benson. I've seen her many times at the house; she is really good friends with Tyson and Terri Steadman. Simone will know if Lenni has any next of kin or if he has a will."

"Thanks, Ella. I'll call Tyson now and ask if they can get hold of Simone. How are you feeling?" asked Gabby.

"Much better, and thanks for all your help today, not sure what I would have done without you."

Tyson and Terri Steadman had moved to Clairemont Island five years previously after a phone call from Tyson's sister Joan, a duty manager at Clairemont Resort. Joan mentioned to Tyson the resort was looking to employ an Entertainments Manager and he'd be perfect for the job.

Tyson had managed his sister Maria's musical career since she had started singing professionally.

He was on a cruise in the middle of the Pacific Ocean when he met Terri for the first time. Maria had a six-month gig singing in the lounge bar from 5:00 p.m. until midnight every night aboard a Carnival Cruise Ship.

One night, quite by chance, Terri sat next to Tyson; he could see she was enjoying singing along with Maria. He was intrigued by her youthful elegance. Her vibrantly dyed red hair stood out most on her tiny frame, but it was her beautiful smile that did it for Tyson, her soft brown eyes just added to her beauty.

When Maria finished for the night he introduced the two of them, and they spent the next few hours getting acquainted. It turned out that Terri had been singing for many years herself, but lacked the confidence to sing in front of an audience. Tyson asked Terri what her favourite song was. She said it was Paul McCartney's *Silly Love Songs*. Maria admitted it was one of her favourite songs as well. Tyson asked them to sing it. They looked at each other, laughed and, with a *what the hell* approach, they sang the song as if they had done it a hundred times before. They were perfect together.

They had such a great time that night, belting out tunes Terri knew the words to.

It got Tyson to thinking and the next day he approached Maria. He wanted to know what she thought about becoming a duet with Terri, their harmony worked perfectly together. Maria loved the idea; between the two of them they had different styles, which would only broaden their audience appeal.

Although Terri had an excellent vocal range for a

lounge musician, she needed more work to confidently sing the required repertoire of 200 variety songs that most bars asked of their musicians.

So, after-hours on the cruise, they worked on a range of songs they were both comfortable in singing, and perfected them until they sang harmoniously in unison.

Over the next few years, Tyson managed both Maria and Terri, along with other musicians. He toured his musicians through USA, Canada and the UK. They sang to sellout crowds in reputable bars and hotel complexes, and while they lived a lucrative life, neither of them was interested in becoming famous. By now, they had met plenty of musicians who made it to the big time overnight and who had succumbed to the extravagant lifestyle of sex, drugs and rock and roll. Many had not lived to tell the tale.

Las Vegas would always hold a special place in their hearts. After years of being on the road together, Tyson and Terri got married in Vegas, but when Joan's call came in, they were thrilled. Their contract was up at the Beat Coffeehouse & Records in downtown Vegas; the timing was perfect. A change of scenery was what they all needed, so Tyson applied for and was successful in getting the job.

The five years they had lived on the island had given them the freedom to start their family. Pregnant with their third child, Terri had her hands full with three-year-old twin boys. She was extremely grateful that she had both Tyson's sisters, Maria and Joan, nearby to help out when needed.

CHAPTER FOURTEEN

Story Of My Life

Gabby apologised for calling Tyson at his home on Sunday afternoon. She explained how Ella had found Lenni's body and that Ella mentioned Terri and Lenni's PA Simone were friends; and could she call around and get their advice on what to do about Lenni?

When Tyson Steadman heard about Lenni's death, he was drawn back to the first time he met Lenni. It was twenty years earlier, when Lenni was part of the band 'Embers' with Eddie Castle and Tommo Gilroy —a heavy metal band following—had brought them fame and fortune, but it didn't last. Lenni's sexual appetite had destroyed the band when he was caught sleeping with backup singer and Eddie's wife, Monica.

Tyson remembered the time with sorrow, even more so now. The demise of a band is always a harrowing time, but way back then, when it happened, it was almost unheard of for a band to break up. The paparazzi relentlessly played it out for months.

Lenni was more suited to rock and roll. He quickly found a niche for himself and it wasn't long before he had a cult following. Writing his own songs was the turning point for Lenni. His first album *Story of my life* sold over a million copies. It was an eclectic mixture of love, hate, misery and fortune. It told the story of his years in the industry.

The number one single from the album *If Only* was dedicated to Monica and portrayed his undying love for his best friend's wife.

The relationship between Eddie and Monica never recuperated. They worked hard to save it for the sake of their children, but the thin thread that fragilely kept them together was permanently ripped apart when the single came out and the paparazzi hounded them ruthlessly.

Eddie was devastated; as far as he was concerned Lenni was scum, but even the scum of the earth didn't do this sort of thing. They hadn't spoken since the day he found Lenni and Monica in bed together.

Eddie's parting words at the time to Lenni were "You contemptible bastard. I never want to see you again. One day, you will get what you deserve and when it happens I'll be the first to stand and applaud."

Lenni hired Reggie Jones as his publicist. Standing comfortably in her 186 cm. slender frame. Reggie dressed to kill. She meant business, and her designer attire reflected exactly that.

She was the catalyst for Lenni's rise to fame and fortune; she called the shots and ran the show.

Reggie took no notice whenever Lenni wanted to slow down or take time out, her objective was to make Lenni a multi-millionaire in the shortest time possible so she could retire young and live the life of her dreams—riding on Lenni's shirttails.

Reggie was the person who leaked the story behind the single *If Only*; knowing the chaos it would unravel would be a small price to pay.

Even though Lenni was thrilled with the success of the album, Eddie was furious to the point of outrage; the paparazzi were like vultures dragging up the past, reliving the demise of his band "Embers" and his marriage. Eddie's hatred for Lenni grew worse by the day; he swore he would get even, he just didn't know how.

The Steadmans lived in a stylish beach house just a block from the resort. Gabby took the opportunity to walk to their house, welcoming the fresh air in an effort to clear her mind and give her some clarity about all that had unfolded throughout the day.

Terri greeted Gabby with a fresh cup of coffee as they sat outside watching the three-year-old twins tear around the backyard on their trikes, banging into anything in the way. Gabby smiled to herself, remembering the joyous times she had recently spent with her grandchildren.

They chatted for ages about Lenni. Both Terri and Tyson shared stories of times spent with him. Terri rang Simone and she picked it up after the third ring, "Hey Terri, thanks for the call, I was going to call to see if you and Ty are free for drinks later today. Seems we will have to stay until after the cyclone. I just got a room at the resort and thought we'd cruise on by after getting settled, if that's OK with you?"

"I didn't realise you were here on the island, when did you arrive? Forget it, tell me all about it when you get here, OK? When do you think that will be?" asked Terri.

"Give us an hour, I'll bring the drinks and something for a barbeque, see you soon," Simone replied.

Gabby expressed her thoughts about the paparazzi trashing the ecological footprint of the island and asked Tyson if he had any ideas on how to deal with the situation.

"I can try to diffuse the situation. We all know how ruthless they are, but when Reggie gets wind of this there will be no stopping her. She's excellent at what she does, but she's driven by the mighty dollar. Trust me, she'll milk this for everything she can. She can only sell his previous albums. It's all old stuff, but I'll lay a million-dollar bet she'll repackage them and make them look like they're new albums. I'm not aware that Lenni's working on anything new, but I'll ask Simone, she will know."

While they waited for Simone and Tommo to arrive, Tyson explained to Gabby what had happened about the demise of the band and what that falling out had been like for everyone.

CHAPTER FIFTEEN

Dirty Little Secrets

Jennifer Robins jolted awake from her sleep. I knew I'd remember who that student was that walked past me into the Glasstop Restaurant, she acknowledged to herself.

Troy Anderson had not been in any of her classes at Melbourne Law School, but he was well known to the faculty. From what Jennifer remembered, he only scraped through university. There was plenty of talk about him and some other students selling exam papers. They were kept under close observation, but the faculty could never prove anything.

She lay there in the darkness trying to fathom how someone with poor grades gets an exclusive position in a New York Law firm. He must have gone through the LLM joint degree program, but to her knowledge, he hadn't. Something didn't add up, of that she was certain.

Jennifer was intrigued enough to make a call to Sarah, she would know.

As an academic, she was fully aware of the A-list students—the faculty spoke of them over lunch, the professors sang their praises, each and every year the faculty knew, within reason, which of their students were going places. It was these A-list students that would be accepted for the LLM joint degree program and, for the life of her, she couldn't recall Troy Anderson as being one of them.

It was widely known that New York University cost a small fortune in tuition; for some, it was in excess of forty thousand US dollars a year; on top of that you have the rising cost of accommodation and general living in New York. How wealthy was his family? Jennifer couldn't remember.

How was he funding this rapid rise up the corporate ladder?

She had to know. Forgetting the time difference, she dialed Sarah's mobile. In truth, she wanted to check up on her friend; she especially wanted to know that Sarah's husband was OK after his fall at work.

"Sarah, I'm so sorry to call you this early, but I wanted to see how Trevor was after his fall. Is everything OK?"

"Morning, Jen. Trevor is a bit battered and bruised; mainly his ego took the brunt of the accident. He's still in the hospital, should be discharged today sometime. How are you going? I hear there is a cyclone heading your way, are you going to be OK, what's the conference like, am I missing anything important?" Sarah tried hard not to sound too envious, she wished she'd gone. Trevor was OK, and he'd have been OK without her there holding his hand.

"Yeah, the conference is amazing, I've got heaps of notes for you, and they are running a conference in Melbourne early next year. I have the dates, actually I've already bought us tickets, but we'll talk about that when I get back.

"I've decided to wait the cyclone out, I really like it here and it looks like these guys have been through this a few times and know what they're doing. I trust that I'll be safe enough here rather than traveling in the midst of it all. I'll let you know how things go or if I change my mind at the last minute."

Then she remembered why she called Sarah. "Sarah, can you remember a student by the name of Troy Anderson? What can you tell me about him— more importantly, do you know if he did the LLM joint degree program?"

"No, I can't recall the name, not sure if he did the program, but I can look it up for you. Why the interest in him?" queried Sarah.

"He's here on the island. I recognised him as soon as I saw him, but couldn't remember his name. What I did remember was his shocking grades and I wondered if he was part of that group that sold exam papers. Remember way back when we suspected a group of students were selling papers, but couldn't prove it?

The ironic thing is that Troy Anderson is here with his family celebrating his upcoming associate position with a New York law firm. I don't know which firm, but I'm wondering how the hell he pulled it off."

"Interesting, I'll go into the office on the way to the hospital to see Trevor and check it out for you.

I'll call you back later today with an update," Sarah responded.

"Thanks, I'd really appreciate it, take care and give my love to Trevor."

Jennifer waited patiently for Sarah to call back; she was curious to see what kind of student he had been, and if her assumptions were correct.

What worried her more was what she would do with the information once she had it.

CHAPTER SIXTEEN

Unconditional Love

Troy had arranged to meet Rose for breakfast early Sunday morning; he wanted to spend quality time with her. He couldn't imagine what his life would be like without Rose in it.

He arrived early and chose a seat slightly secluded from the rest of the patrons. He didn't want anyone listening to their conversation. He knew he had no choice. To save what he could of their special relationship, he had to tell her the truth before she heard it from someone else.

From where he was seated he could see Rose approach the café. Struggling slightly with the wind, she remained composed; her silky long brown hair bounced off her shoulders with every step, her radiant smile was breath-taking. He could tell that Rose, regardless of what was happening around her, was taking in the beauty of the scenery.

Troy stood to welcome her, the tender hug may have lingered a moment longer than necessary, but only he was aware of that.

"I'm in love with this place, it's amazing, so beautiful and serene even with the inclement weather, and everyone is lovely and helpful. Are you having a good time?" Rose asked

"Certainly, such a wondrous island full of many exotic creatures; I'll be sad to leave," Troy said.

"On that note, you'll never guess whom I met last night."

Rose shook her head in anticipation. "No idea. Who?"

"Lenni Maxwell. Remember, I went to uni with him. We were in a few classes together until he got kicked out. Not that he needed an education, with a voice like his. We spent hours last night talking about the good old days. He's got an Australasian tour coming up next month, did you know about it?"

"No, it's not something I would have paid any attention to, with the move to Hong Kong. His music is OK, but I wouldn't call myself a fan." Rose dismissed the conversation as she scanned the breakfast menu.

As the waitress took their order, Troy asked the waitress to take a photo of them, as he wanted to remember this moment forever. He wanted to capture her beauty and hold it in his heart for a lifetime. He doubted very much if she would ever look at him in the same way again, when she knew what he had done.

Hours passed far too quickly. Rose was excited about her new job. She had gone to the Faculty of Dentistry at the University of Hong Kong, so she was very familiar with the city.

She imagined it wouldn't have changed much in

the three years she'd been working in Australia. Thankfully, she still had friends living there. As she gazed off into the distance, she thoughtfully reminisced about the good times.

Rose was the first to mention the need to get back to the resort to pack. Their parents had expressed the urgency to get off the island before the cyclone hit.

Troy didn't want to leave—he knew he had to tell Rose the truth, but didn't know how. He didn't want to break his connection with her, but now that he suspected he'd been caught, he didn't know what was to become of his future.

He wasn't looking forward to the move to New York. Sure it was an amazing opportunity, but it was his father's dream, not his. Troy didn't need the requisite pretentious lifestyle, although he would benefit from the remuneration package offered. In truth, he didn't want to be so far away from Rose.

There was also a more troubling consideration; could he actually perform the work to the standard required? After all, he had managed to con his way through his career progression so far. Going to New York and working for the big punters was a totally new ball game; this would be the big league and there would be no survivors—he'd either crash and burn, or miraculously fumble through, as he'd been able to do until now, but was the risk worth it?

If he was perfectly honest with himself, sex had gotten him to where he was today; he'd slept his way to the top, and he wasn't ashamed to admit it.

Legal secretaries and grad students would do anything if they thought it would get them a step closer, and he used and abused them every step of the way.

Until now no one knew of his secret passions, secret thoughts, secret desires. This trip to Clairemont Island had, for the first time ever, brought his past into his present and he wasn't happy with the way it was progressing. He was damn sure it wasn't going to be the death of him; he had too much to lose.

He didn't regret his decision to put an end to the voice that threatened him. The way in which he did it could have been better executed, but in the heat of the moment, that's how it all unfolded.

As Rose and Troy walked back to Clairemont Resort, both lost in their own thoughts. Rose, of her friends in Hong Kong and Troy trying to find the words he needed to reveal the truth to her. The words that ran around and around his head still refusing to come forth.

As a crash of thunder broke the silence, the rain shattered the moment as they ran for the safety of the resort.

Drenched in rain, Rose disappeared to her room before Troy could compose himself. Without further ado, he knew what he had to do next. It was now or never.

CHAPTER SEVENTEEN

On Reflection

Simone Benson and Tommo Gilroy arrived at Terri and Tyson's home within the hour. As Tyson handed out drinks he introduced Gabby.

"Do you come to the island often?" Gabby asked.

"Not every time Lenni comes, but I have been here a lot lately. Lenni is working on some things that need my attention. Tommo and I were sailing around the islands when we heard about the cyclone and made our way here to catch up with everyone while we waited the cyclone out."

"When did you arrive?" Terri asked.

"We arrived on Friday afternoon, and we had drinks with Lenni Friday night," Simone responded.

Gabby, Terri and Tyson paused for a moment looking at each other. Not sure who was going to break the news. In the end, Tyson took the plunge.

"Simone, Tommo," he paused, unable to find the words. "Lenni's dead, they found his body this morning."

Simone now a deathly shade of white, stammered: "No, that can't be true, is it some kind of joke?" But the look on Terri and Tyson's face said it all, no more words were necessary as she succumbed to tears.

Full of composure, Gabby tried to comfort everyone "It's not a joke. Ella, his cleaner, found him. She called Dr. Scott who went up to the house and gave Ella a sedative, the poor girl was hysterical. Then he called me to bring the head of security and our photographer.

"We've spoken to mainland police who say they can't get here until after the cyclone, which could be five days away, depending on how bad we are hit."

Gabby continued, "When we were going through Lenni's house looking for important documentation to identify any next of kin, we couldn't find any; then Ella mentioned that you guys were friends, which is why I'm here. I called to ask Terri for your number. We both agreed that you would probably know of any family to contact."

Simone and Tommo looked at each other and shook their heads; neither of them knew of any family that Lenni had. It seemed the conversation had never come up over all these years. Although Lenni was a public figure, he was a very private person. His parents had passed away many years ago and as an only child they were not aware of any other living relatives.

"We weren't sure whom to contact about his death. We thought if he had personal papers you would know where he stores them. His lawyer would know if he has a will. Do you know who his lawyer is?" Gabby asked.

Simone nodded her head, "Yes, he uses a firm in

Hong Kong; the lawyer's contact details are on my phone, and I'll write them down for you."

"Simone, we are trying to keep it out of the press for now, no point in giving the paparazzi a head start on the witch-hunt that is pretty much guaranteed. Can we get your assurance that you will keep it quiet for now?"

"Yes, of course, we will," Tommo assured them. "But you haven't told us how he died. If you want us to keep it quiet you must suspect his death is murder. Is that what you are thinking?"

"We have no idea yet how he died—just that he was found face down in the pool. It may have been an accident or someone may have done something to him. We'll have to wait for Dr. Scott to get back to us about that."

"In the meantime, I thought it would be helpful to gather a picture of what he was up to from his arrival on the island on Thursday until he was found on Sunday morning. Who he talked to and what his state of mind was. If we can build that into something before mainland police arrive, then we may just solve it before the paparazzi gets wind of it."

"Great idea," said Simone, "I'm all for keeping the paparazzi out of it. They will be all over the island like a rash."

"Reggie will milk this for everything it's worth. Has anyone contacted her yet?"

"No, we wanted to speak to you first," Tyson interjected.

Visibly still shaken, Simone accepted another cup of coffee. Gabby asked what time they had met with Lenni on Friday night.

With both hands around the cup, Simone looked into the liquid as though searching for answers. "It was around 6:00 p.m. because Lenni had to leave for a meeting with someone at 8:00 p.m. and before you ask, no I don't know who he was meeting. I didn't think to ask."

"What was his state of mind? Gabby asked.

Tommo jumped in, allowing Simone to gather her thoughts. "He was fine; I'd say he was normal. Admittedly, he wasn't expecting us, but he took the time to meet with us regardless. He was so excited about his new album coming out—it would be ready for marketing in time for his Australasian tour next month."

Tyson interjected: "I wasn't aware that Lenni was working on a new album. I spoke to him just last month and he didn't mention a thing."

"I was sworn to secrecy, he was keeping it pretty hush, hush," Simone shared.

"This new album is a continuum of his life as a musician. From what I can gather, he names people in this album. I heard him arguing with Reggie about it. They were having one hell of an argument. Apparently, Lenni had dropped one of the tracks, but he found out that Reggie had included it into the album before sending it off for distribution. By the time Lenni found out it was too late.

I heard Reggie shouting at him; "If you didn't want people to know about it then why did you write a song about it and why would you record it? It's too late now anyway, and what does it matter, it'll make us millions."

CHAPTER EIGHTEEN

Secret Rendezvous

Grant Woodham was furious. Since Lenni had stormed away from him in the parking lot, Grant had spent every moment on the phone trying to fix the rift Lenni had caused. Grant refused to admit defeat; there had to be another way, and he knew there was only one person left who could save them all.

"Susan, hi it's Grant. My plans fell through for tonight. I know we were going to hook up later for drinks, but if you're free now, I'd love to see you."

Grant waited patiently as he heard Susan rustle papers. "Sure thing, I've done enough paperwork for one day, shall I come to your room?" Susan asked, as she turned off her computer ready to leave the office.

"Yes, come to my room, we'll order in like last night if you want. See you soon." Two years ago, on the mainland, quite by chance, Grant met Susan for the first time. Seated opposite at different tables, they couldn't help but notice each other, as they both waited patiently for their own guests to arrive. Neither arrived and after an hour of waiting Grant, feeling sorry for her, asked if she would like to join him for dinner. She accepted and they hit it off.

They spent all evening talking about their work, their interests and their struggles. After the third bottle of wine Susan agreed to move the conversation up to her room in the hotel.

After that weekend together their hunger for each other was insatiable—they felt like sex-starved teenagers. They knew it was wrong, but neither gave a damn, they clicked like they'd been together forever.

Grant was already divorced at that stage, but he was concerned about Susan's home life. He knew her daughter Emily was very important to her, but she hardly talked about Dwayne, her husband. He wasn't sure if their relationship was worth salvaging, or what was going to happen there.

After a year of secret rendezvous on the mainland or at Clairemont Resort, he knew their relationship was more than just a fling. He wasn't entirely sure how she felt about it. Regardless, he supported her decision to keep their affair quiet and not be seen together, and he was more than happy to grab a hotel room anytime they could hook up.

If he was honest with himself, he had already fallen in love with her before he knew about Coastal Developments latest project, which turned out to be the development on Clairemont Island. He put his hand up to oversee the project, knowing it would give him and Susan more time together.

What he didn't realise when he began overseeing the project was Susan's involvement. When he explained the project to her, he embellished quite a lot; he was desperate to get her on board. Without realising it, Susan, by default, would become a very intricate player—not that she would ever know.

Susan was not stupid. When Grant revealed the project and asked if she would sell the condos through her real estate business, she could see the potential and knew in no uncertain terms this would be the making of her and her business.

Oh, what she could do with the money! Thoughts raced through her head: she could ditch her husband once and for all. Hell, she could even move off the island altogether and live a life of luxury in Bali, like she had always dreamed of.

Having an affair with Grant so close to home was a small price to pay for the hefty commissions coming her way. The plans of the development looked amazing, they would be easy to offload, and it looked like the Coastal Developments Group was legit and had all the paperwork under control.

Susan had nothing to worry about, it would be smooth sailing, or so she thought.

Susan was taken aback when Grant asked her if she would cosy up to Lenni and get him onside with the deal. Not a problem with that, she thought; she was a massive fan, so any excuse to spend time with him was OK in her books.

Grant set up a meeting with Lenni and introduced Susan to him, explaining to Lenni that Susan's real estate agency was going to be selling the condos.

All three raised their champagne glasses as they toasted the success of the development. All three would get into bed together, so to speak. Grant didn't realise that, over time, Lenni and Susan actually would get into bed together, but if it meant the development would go ahead without any glitches, then who was he to rock the boat? He did the only thing he could, he turned a blind eye.

But after the confronting meeting, or rather lack of meeting with Lenni, he knew he was going to have to call on Susan to make Lenni understand what his pulling out of the deal would do to all their careers. He was thrilled that Susan could come and see him earlier than expected.

Susan arrived, entered Grant's hotel room and filled it with a breath of fresh air. She looked radiant, relaxed and refreshed, and you would never know she had just finished a twelve-hour day at the office. Grant handed her a glass of wine. Thankfully, room service had already delivered their lobster salad. Once seated opposite Grant, Susan took a moment to catch her breath; it had been a long arduous day for her, but that's the price you pay when you own your own business.

Gazing into Grant's eyes, she felt as though she had met her soul mate. There was a familiarity beyond their physical attraction to each other; it was as if they had been together in another lifetime. She would do anything for him.

She wasn't ashamed to admit to herself that all the times she lay in bed with Lenni, she was doing it for the future—for her and Grant. Lenni was a skilled lover and she probably enjoyed their lovemaking more than she should, but she had to act like she was committed to both relationships in order to get what she wanted from this development.

Far too often she told herself that it was OK to make love to both Grant and Lenni. She was doing it for the security of her future, and the chance to move with Grant to Bali, where they had carefully planned a life of luxury. There was no denying she actually believed that.

She didn't, couldn't, or wouldn't think about what would happen to her marriage to Dwayne or how the relationship with her daughter Emily would turn out. That thought was so far removed it almost didn't exist.

Grant wasn't about to ruin their rendezvous by bringing up Lenni, so he enjoyed a leisurely meal with Susan, admitting to himself he was desperately in love with her.

They made love fully and without regret, and as they rested snuggled in each other's arms Grant made mention of his meeting with Lenni.

Susan's reaction surprised him; she was furious. "How could you let him pull out of the deal?" she wailed.

"I didn't. I mean haven't yet, he's confused, he doesn't know what he wants. I think we should go to his house and talk to him, answer any of his questions and find out what's really going on. What do you think?" he asked Susan.

"Yeah, I reckon you're right. Let's go and find out. It's still early, I'm sure he'll still be up. Why don't I call him and ask if I can come up? He'll think it's just going to be me, chances are he'll be OK with that," Susan nervously suggested.

Calling Lenni late at night was a regular occurrence for Susan, knowing Lenni liked his affairs kept private. Susan tried to downplay it in the hope that Grant didn't catch on to the fact she'd done this more often than she'd already revealed to him.

Susan picked up her mobile and dialed Lenni; he answered on the third ring.

"Hiya sexy, when you coming over? I've been waiting for you." Lenni slurred into his phone. Music was blaring in the background, she could hardly make out what he was saying, and then she remembered his party.

"I'll be there soon, who's still there?" she asked cautiously.

"Come on, sexy, I really want you, are you coming?"

"Yes, I'm coming now, but who is with you, how many people are still at your party?" She shouted to be heard over the music.

"I'm not su...re, I don....t know, I don't want theeeemmm, I want you. Come over now." Although the slurring of his words and the loud music made it difficult to understand what he was saying, she got it loud and clear that he wanted to see her, so that was a good thing.

"Yes, Lenni, I'll be there soon; why don't you tell everyone to go home, you don't want them seeing me there, do you?"

"Stuff 'em, Suze, who cares?" Deep down, Susan knew that Lenni cared; it was just the booze talking.

"Sorry, Grant, I can't seem to get out of him how many people are still at his place. I totally forgot he was having a party tonight. Tell you what, why don't I go up and talk to him? Then, if I don't get any satisfaction, I'll call you and together we'll try, does that sound like a plan?"

"Yeah, sure thing. It's best you do it, he's already told me no. You may get a better outcome," Grant said reassuringly.

Susan showered and dressed. All the while Grant kept wondering how this was going to pan out; what would Susan say to Lenni that would get him to change his mind?

If Susan couldn't get Lenni to change his mind, what would he be forced to do to save face with the Coastal Developments Board and secure his job?

CHAPTER NINETEEN

A Shift Of Energy

As Gabby woke on Monday morning, she could feel the energy of the island had shifted, even before she pulled the curtains. Looking outside the air felt dense and the dark clouds seemed to emit an eerie, sinister tension.

This does not look good she thought to herself. Is the island preparing itself for a mammoth cyclone or is the death of Lenni hanging its curse over the island?

Gabby paused over her coffee, pondering what the universe was warning her of.

A normal person would look at the dark clouds and immediately put them down to the incoming cyclone. Gabby, however, was not a normal person— her intuition was drawn to Lenni, she wondered if his death was accidental or was a murderer lurking on the island?

If so, who was it who killed him, and why? She had so many scenarios rolling around in her head, but none of it made any sense to her.

Time to call on some friends, she thought. Michael was hanging up the phone as she poured her second cup of coffee: "That was the Mayor; he wanted to make sure we were working with the cyclone readiness team. He seems a touch apprehensive, I had to remind him we've all been through this many times before and even though we don't know what the heavens will deliver, we have to trust that the locals know exactly what they're doing. I reassured him that we'd do another cyclone briefing with the guests today, just to keep him happy."

"Michael, I have a real uneasy feeling in the pit of my stomach, and I know it's about Lenni's death. I'm going to see if Scotty and James can find a few minutes today to start brainstorming everything we've got, and I'd love you to be there as well." Even as she said it, her gut was turning somersaults.

"Of course. I don't have anything on today apart from making sure the resort is 100% cyclone ready, but I trust the staff to implement all the systems, so I'm ready whenever you are." The fear in Gabby's eyes said it all.

"Scotty, Gabby here, can you spare me a few minutes today? I want to go through all the information we have on Lenni's death, something just doesn't feel right and I'm not sure what I'm missing. Thought we could do a brainstorming session if you have the time."

After a quick flick through his diary, Scotty replied, "I can be there around 11:00 a.m. if that's OK?"

"Come to our apartment, Scotty. I'll ask James and Michael to join us."

"Michael, it's 11:00 a.m., can you please call into the security office and ask James to join us, I'm sure he will have his own thoughts on Lenni's death."

After Michael left to do the rounds of the resort and to check in with James, Gabby went and grabbed a whiteboard from her office and made her way back to her apartment.

Totally lost in her own thoughts, she didn't see Andrew, manager of Zanzabar, until she banged into him.

"Sorry, Andrew, I didn't see you, are you OK?"

"Yes, Ms. Saintclaire, I'm fine. Looks like you're miles away, are you OK?"

"Yes, Andrew, I've got loads on my mind and I'm so sorry to have banged into you."

"That's perfectly fine, haven't you heard the old saying *a problem shared is a problem halved*? Is there something I can help you with?" Andrew asked his boss.

"You're going to hear soon enough, Andrew, but please don't reveal this to anyone else as it's still a massive secret for now. The truth is that Lenni Maxwell died and it looks suspiciously like murder, although we don't have confirmation on that yet. I'm waiting to hear from Dr. Scott.

Mainland police can't get here until after the cyclone and if it is murder, the murderer could be anyone, even a guest here in our resort. The thought sends shivers up my spine."

"Wow, that's serious news. I promise I won't say anything," Andrew replied as he wandered back to work.

CHAPTER TWENTY

Karma

As Andrew walked back to the Zanzabar, the encounter with Troy on Friday night kept playing around and around in his head. Could Troy have murdered Lenni? They went to uni together, and they certainly had a shady past, but would he, could he, murder someone? Andrew didn't think so, but he suspected Troy was hiding something. He didn't know what Troy was mixed up in; he assumed it must be pretty bad—Troy had admitted as much.

When he got back to the bar, he picked up the phone and called Gabby.

"Ms. Saintclaire, do you have a moment, I wanted to talk to you about Lenni, perhaps somewhere quiet?"

"Yes, of course, Andrew. Come to my apartment now if you want. Is there someone else on the bar to cover for you?"

Andrew agreed in response and added a reluctant: "See you soon."

Gabby wasn't sure what Andrew wanted to talk to her about, so decided not to call James. She would wait until he had arrived and ask if he wanted James to be present. She popped on a fresh pot of coffee and was pleased to see that Michael hadn't eaten all the blueberry muffins she had made earlier that day.

Andrew arrived with an air of apprehension; she could tell he had something on his mind. She invited him to sit as she poured coffee for them both. Allowing him the freedom to start the conversation, she didn't want to appear intrusive, after all, he was the one who had approached her.

"Ms. Saintclaire, it's about a friend of mine, Troy Anderson. When I say a friend of mine, I mean we went to university together, but I hadn't seen him for eight years until he walked into the Zanzabar on Friday night.

"Troy started to tell me what he'd been up to over those years, but the bar got busy and he didn't reveal anything. I knew something was up. He said if anyone found out about what he was really like he'd go down like a ball of flames, his reputation would be shot and his family would disown him. Something was really troubling him.

"I heard that he was with Lucy at Lenni's party. The twins Faith and Fay told me they saw him going through all the rooms like he was searching for something. They said he was acting pretty suspiciously. After what has happened, I just thought you should know. That's all."

"I appreciate you being honest with me, Andrew. It must have been a tough decision for you to make, letting me know, that is, and I'm sure it's nothing, but I'll make a mental note of it anyway."

Gabby felt uneasiness in the pit of her stomach. This didn't sound like the actions of the young man she had met just a few days prior. Rita and Stan Anderson had portrayed their son as an all-round good guy, the boy-next-door persona.

What was he looking for, she wondered. What possessed him to go through each room—that puzzled her.

Gabby remembered Ella had mentioned that Lucy and Troy had spent hours outside talking to Lenni. Ella alluded to the fact they were probably talking business, but what business would that be, she wondered. I must ask Lucy what they talked about out by the pool; that may give me some insight into what Troy was up to.

As Andrew made his way back to the Zanzabar, he felt a sense of relief—after what had happened in uni, he felt very little loyalty toward Troy. "If this is karma coming to bite you in the bum, then I hope it takes a bloody big chunk," Andrew muttered to himself.

CHAPTER TWENTY-ONE

Ulterior Motives

"There were scratches on his shoulders and bruising around his neck. It appears someone tried to strangle him, but that wasn't what killed him. It was the blunt trauma to the back of the head. Indicating someone hit him from behind.

He was already dead before his body entered the pool. Which indicates Lenni was murdered.

So far his toxicology report has shown traces of alcohol and cocaine. It would take a few more days to show more specific drugs. From what we have seen at his house and the stories we have heard, can we think of anyone who would want to kill Lenni?" Scotty asked.

"Eddie Castle has to be a suspect, he has motive, as does his ex-wife, Monica," Gabby revealed.

"Who is Eddie Castle?" Michael asked.

Gabby gave them an update on her visit to Tyson and Terri's home and her conversation with Simone and Tommo.

"I spoke to Simone and Tommo, but they have no idea where Eddie is right now, they haven't spoken to him in years. Simone did reveal that Lenni was about to release a new album and we all know what happened when his last album was released—all hell broke loose and Eddie declared Lenni would get what was coming to him. Maybe Eddie found out about this new album and wanted to silence Lenni beforehand."

"What about Monica, Eddie's ex-wife?" James interjected. "Maybe she was scared she would be named in this new album. Maybe she wanted to get even with Lenni for ruining her life."

James glanced over to Gabby. "How can we find out where they both were on Saturday night or early Sunday morning?"

"That's something D.I. Reid would organise. I'll give her a call," Gabby said.

"Scotty, do you have any idea of the time of death? Gabby asked.

"No, not yet. I don't know for certain, but I would guesstimate it to be sometime between midnight and six o'clock Sunday morning."

"What else do we know that could be relevant to this investigation?" Gabby asked.

James told them that he had called most of the people from the list of names Ella had given him. "I didn't say why I was calling, just that someone had put a complaint in about the party, and I was following up on who was there and the times they arrived and left, and if they saw anything unusual that night. Their stories are pretty similar. But, I can't pinpoint the last person to leave the party."

"Apparently Lenni spent most of the night outside

talking. Ella spent most of the time making sure that people didn't trash the place; she was in her normal housekeeping mode. Ella told me that Lucy arrived with a cute looking guy that she hadn't seen before —who I now believe is a guest of ours, Troy Anderson. They spent a few hours outside talking to Lenni, but Ella didn't see them leave."

"The twins, Faith and Faye, told me that a cute looking guy was opening up all the doors as if he was looking for something or someone. They were going to follow him, but then Dwayne Olsen, the football coach, started chatting them up and they got caught up with that and forgot all about this other guy. I wonder if he is the same person that Lucy took to the party."

James nodded. "He could be. Kathy O'Connor told me that Dwayne's wife has been having an affair with Lenni; seems Kathy found that out while at the party, and she told Dwayne. Apparently he was angry, but not angry enough to have it out with Lenni. Instead, he moved in on the twins, and they didn't seem to object."

"Dwayne Olsen has just had a heart attack; are you sure it was him?" asked Gabby.

James nodded in agreement, then suggested they put Dwayne on the suspect list; he certainly had motive.

She asked Michael to check with housekeeping to see if Lucy was still on duty or if she had finished for the day.

"She's finished for the day. Shall I call her at home and ask her about her movements on Saturday night?" asked James.

James called Lucy, and she was happy enough to

come back to the resort.

"I'm not quite sure how Lucy would know Troy. Why don't we just ask Lucy if she attended Lenni's party and see what she reveals? If she doesn't mention the guy she took, then we'll have to find another way of getting to the answer. After all, there were plenty of people at the party; someone will be sure to know."

They didn't have to wait long before Lucy tapped quietly on the door. She looked around the room upon entering and wondered what she had done wrong. Why was she called to the boss's apartment? Had there been a complaint put in about her? She took great pride in her work; therefore she couldn't understand why her cleaning would be in question.

Maybe someone had complained about her sexual encounters with the guests, but they seemed pretty happy with what they were getting—she couldn't for one moment think she'd been caught out in that respect.

"Hello, Ms. Saintclaire, is there something I can help you with?" Lucy asked as she desperately tried to read the faces around the room.

"Lucy, I'm not sure you are aware, but there has been a complaint put in about Lenni's party on Saturday night, and we're wondering if you can tell us what you know about it or the people who were there.

"If you would rather not say anything at all, that's perfectly fine."

"No, that's OK, I have nothing to hide. I went to the party, arrived about eight and left sometime around eleven o'clock, I think. Sorry, I can't be more specific, I didn't look at the time. I know I arrived just after 8:00 p.m. because I picked up one of the guests from the resort at eight." Lucy started to feel more relaxed knowing it wasn't anything she had done that had her called into the boss's apartment.

"Lucy, did you notice anything unusual happen at the party, or was there anyone there you didn't know?" James asked cautiously. He didn't want to put her on edge, but decided to slowly bring Troy into the conversation.

"No, I don't recall anyone new there, I'm not really sure because I didn't really look around. Apart from getting a glass of water in the kitchen, I didn't even go inside.

"I walked from the front door right out back to the pool because I knew that's where Lenni would be."

Lucy was adamant she hadn't noticed anything unusual, but now she wasn't sure, she'd have to give it more thought.

"Lucy, do you have any idea how many people were there when you left? Can you remember who they were?" questioned Gabby.

"I'm not sure, I wasn't really paying attention. I had a massive headache and just wanted to get out of there, the noise was killing me. I was in the kitchen when I yelled out to Troy if he wanted to get a lift back to the resort and he said yeah, he had a headache as well. For some reason, Lenni had the music up far too loud; I reckon the whole island could have heard it. I drove Troy back to the resort, but to be honest I'm not sure of the time. As I said, my head was pounding."

James decided to take the lead. "Lucy may I ask how you came to invite Troy to the party? We are talking about Troy Anderson, the guest in room

1208?"

"Yes, that's him. When I was cleaning his room, he asked what there was to do on the island at night, and I mentioned I was going to a party and asked if he'd like to join me. He said that would be great, and so I picked him up at 8:00 p.m. and we drove up to Lenni's place."

"Did Troy enjoy himself at the party?" Gabby asked.

"Yes, I suppose so; he didn't know whose party it was until we got there. It's funny how things work out; but it happened that Troy and Lenni went to university together, so they already knew each other. They had a couple of beers each as they chatted about old times, but I think Lenni said something that pissed Troy off. I can't recall what was said. To be honest, I wasn't paying any attention to either of them. By then I had a headache and I just sipped my beer and gazed into the pool while they chatted."

Just as Gabby was going to ask another question, Lucy butted in, saying that Troy had stormed off in a huff and he disappeared into the house. She was about to follow him when Lenni started talking about other things. It was probably thirty minutes before she managed to get away from Lenni and find Troy again.

"Thanks, Lucy, you've been very helpful. That's all for now. I appreciate you coming back in after leaving work," Gabby said as she showed Lucy to the door.

"Although Troy seemed to be acting suspiciously, I'm not sure this makes him a murderer. Lucy said she drove him back to the resort, so unless he drove back to Lenni's by himself, then it can't have been him."

James and Scotty nodded in agreement, "I suppose the only way we will know for sure is if we call Troy in and ask him. What do you all think?" Michael added.

"Yes, I suppose you are right," Gabby responded as she picked up the phone to call Troy's room. He answered the phone on the third ring; the movie he was watching had just finished and he was contemplating what to do next.

CHAPTER TWENTY-TWO

Second Chances

"Hello, Mr. Anderson, it's Gabby Saintclaire, Manager of Clairemont Resort. You are not in any trouble, but I believe you may have been a guest at Lenni Maxwell's party on Saturday night. There have been some complaints about that party and we are speaking to everyone who attended. I'm wondering if I could ask you some questions about what you saw that night. Would that be OK with you?"

"Yes, Ms. Saintclaire. I was at Lenni's party, but I wasn't there that long and to be honest I didn't talk to anyone other than Lenni and the person who took me, so not sure I can be of any help to you," Troy rather sheepishly replied.

"Mr. Anderson, if you could spare us just a few minutes I'd be very grateful, something may jog your memory. If it's OK, can I ask you to come to my apartment? I will send James, our head of security, to escort you. I assure you that you aren't in any trouble."

"Yeah, OK, send him over," Troy consented.

As Troy waited he thought back to the party, and wondered if someone had seen him taking cocaine. Hell, everyone was having their share, so why shouldn't he? Lenni had told him to help himself, so he hadn't stolen anything, he was offered it and it would have been rude for him not to partake.

James was there in a couple of minutes. Troy closed the door behind him, making sure it locked, before he was escorted down the corridor to Gabby's apartment.

James didn't utter a word to Troy as they walked the three-minute journey.

Upon entering the apartment, he was taken aback by the people seated at the dining table. As he sat at the indicated seat, Gabby introduced him to Dr. Scott, James and Michael. She offered him coffee, which he declined, and then he looked around the room, wondering who was going to start the conversation.

"Mr. Anderson, thanks for coming. I trust we haven't intruded upon your activities today." Gabby started.

"No, that's OK, I wasn't doing anything important," Troy answered.

"As I mentioned on the phone, there has been a complaint about Lenni's party and we are asking those that attended their version of what they saw and who they spoke to that night. Would you be able to tell us how you came to know about the party and what you observed from the moment you arrived until the time you left?" Gabby sounded more in control than she felt.

"Firstly, I don't want to get anyone into trouble, but I asked my cleaner if there was anything exciting to do on the island. She said she was going to a party that night and I was welcome to join her. I don't want to mention her name because I'm not sure she's allowed to invite guests to parties and I don't want to get her into any trouble. But she took me to Lenni's party.

She didn't say where we were going and I couldn't even tell you where it was, but I knew him because we went to uni together. We sat and talked for an hour or so and then we left."

Gabby looked around the room and realised they were allowing her to continue the questioning. "Did you notice anything suspicious inside the house, or was anyone acting suspiciously. Was there any fighting or arguments that you were aware of?" Gabby continued.

"No, I didn't see anything that looked suspicious to me, nobody was arguing, but I didn't know anyone there apart from Lenni and the cleaner who took me," Troy responded.

"It must have been great to catch up with Lenni. When was the last time you saw each other?"

"Not since uni, so yes, it was nice to catch up on all that he's done. Mind you, I read the papers so know pretty much everything he's been up to anyway."

"I believe Lucy took you to the party, and no she won't get in any trouble. Was Lucy with you the entire time you were at Lenni's house?" Gabby enquired.

Troy took a moment to unravel how he was going to explain his actions inside the house. Had someone seen him going through all the rooms and complained about it? He wasn't even sure what the complaint was, so decided to ask. After all, he was a lawyer, best he start defending himself.

"Before I answer your questions, please tell me what the complaint is and who it's against." Troy knew he was fishing; he also knew none of them would have any legal cognizance.

James took it upon himself to answer: "May I call you Troy?"

"Yes, that's fine, please continue." Troy lowered his open hand offering the floor to the security guy.

James looked over Troy's head and caught sight of Gabby and Michael, who both nodded in agreement, acknowledging that James could reveal the death of Lenni.

"Troy, it's like this; Lenni was killed early on Sunday morning and we are talking to everyone who attended the party. We want to keep this as quiet as possible, so we actually haven't yet told any of the guests that he's dead. Please keep this to yourself. As you are aware, there is a cyclone coming and the island has enough to worry about without wondering who the murderer may be."

The shocked expression on Troy's face was all that Gabby needed; she quickly reassured Troy that he wasn't a suspect. She asked quite innocently: "Troy, you were observed storming off in a huff from Lenni and then you were seen going through all the rooms inside his house. Can you explain what happened with Lenni and why were you going through the rooms—what were you looking for?"

"Lenni and I were in uni together and yes we liked to party. In fact, Lenni was expelled from uni in his first year. I haven't seen him since then, but it didn't stop him from dragging up the past and, to be honest, it hurt to remember what we got up to. When I asked him to let it go, he wouldn't, and so I decided to go for a pee. I wouldn't say I stormed off, I was bursting and needed to go to the toilet.

"Yes, I looked through each of the rooms because the music was too loud and I wanted to turn it down. It was giving me a headache and I'd had some beers; trust me, the two don't go down well together. That's all, no biggie. I just wanted to turn the music down, that's all."

"Thanks for that, I appreciate your honesty. Do you know what time you left the party, and can you remember how many people would have still been there?" James asked.

"It was early, not sure exactly what time, my head was pounding, but I reckon it was around 11:00 p.m."

"Troy, where was Lenni when you left?" Michael asked.

"No, can't help you with that one. Lenni was outside and I didn't get back out there. Lucy came looking for me and we left through the front door. There were people in the lounges, but I didn't see outside; I couldn't tell you if Lenni was still out there or not."

"Thanks for your time Troy, you've been a great help, and if you can keep this under your belt, we would be extremely grateful." Gabby re-affirmed as she extended her hand to his shoulder in a sympathetic gesture.

"Yeah, sure thing. I mean, it's quite unnerving to think Lenni has been murdered. If I can be of any assistance in helping you out, I'm happy to offer my legal knowledge, but then I'm sure you must have many lawyers here on the island," Troy contributed.

"Thanks for your offer, Troy. I'll take that into consideration, and no we don't have any lawyers here on the island, so your offer is greatly appreciated," James said as he shook his hand in acceptance.

"Actually, strike that," Troy blurted.

"I don't understand, strike what?" James asked.

"Strike my offer of legal help; I'm not even sure I'm a lawyer anymore," Troy said. "Before I do anything else, I need to talk to Jennifer Robins to determine my future."

Troy slumped into a chair as a confused audience watched in silence. He took a moment for the realisation to sink in.

Then he explained about the chance encounter with Jennifer Robins as he was rushing out to meet Rose for breakfast early Sunday morning.

"Ah, Mr. Anderson, just the person I wanted to speak to," Jennifer Robins yelled out across the foyer; she wanted to talk to Troy before he headed out of the resort.

"Sorry, can I help you?" Troy asked. He recognised the face, but couldn't put a name to it.

"I'm Dr. Jennifer Robins, from Melbourne Law School. I happened to overhear that you have been appointed an associate position in New York. What a wonderful achievement, you must be thrilled?"

"Yes, I am, why?" Troy quietly asked.

"It's just that I was speaking to Dr. Sarah Dyer, remember her? She is on the board of the LLM joint degree program with New York University. We had a very interesting conversation about you.

"Would you like to join me for a coffee so I can reveal what that conversation was about?" Jennifer knew she had him by the balls; there was no escaping it now.

Knowing exactly where this was going, Troy willingly agreed. His past had caught up with him, and, to be honest, he felt relieved.

"Sure thing," he said as he followed her into the Blissful Retreat Coffee Shop.

"I've heard some very damning reports about you, Mr. Anderson. It appears you were cautioned and put under suspicion for selling exam papers. A transcript of your final grades is being emailed to me as we speak, but I already know the results are pathetic. You did not get into the LLM joint degree program, so how is it that you came to be accepted into a New York Law firm?" Jennifer asked curiously.

Troy sat for a moment in quiet contemplation. He was tired of lying, sick of running from his past. It was time to tell the truth, time to make amends, and time he told his parents, it was now or never.

"You are perfectly correct. Yes, I am guilty of all that. And how did I get here? I've slept my way to the top. My father bought me the associate position. To be honest, I don't want the job. I don't want to move to New York. You have done me a huge favour by bringing this out now. You have saved me from a fate worse than death."

Jennifer could tell he was a defeated soul; the look on his face spoke volumes. Jennifer sat there in stunned silence, trying to take in what had just happened. She knew he meant everything he had just said, his expression could not lie.

"What are you going to do about it?" Jennifer asked.

"I'm going to confront my parents and tell them the truth. I need to be set free." And with that Troy rose from *the table; he bent forward and kissed Jennifer on the forehead.*

"Did you confront your parents?" James asked.

"No, I went to breakfast with my sister Rose. I wanted to tell her the truth first, we have an amazing relationship and I wanted her to be the first to know. The only trouble was I couldn't bring myself to tell her, I couldn't find the right words, so decided I had to face my parents first."

Troy was a broken man. Gabby could feel his anguish as he recalled the encounter with his parents.

He was reluctant to admit that Jennifer held his future in her hands. For him to move forward, he knew they would have to meet; he couldn't put it off any longer.

"I'll let you know the outcome," he mumbled as he stood to leave.

Gabby moved forward, she wanted to reassure him that the universe sometimes works in mysterious ways; she prayed for him that this was one of those times.

CHAPTER TWENTY-THREE

Hidden Clues

Gabby shook her head, struggling to remember all the facts that now presented themselves.

"I thought it must have been Troy, but now that I've met him and listened to what he has to say, I'm not sure. What do you guys think?" she asked, but the dumbfounded looks on their faces told her they had no clues either.

"Sorry, Gabby, I have to get back to the Medical Centre," Scotty announced.

"That's OK, I need a break anyway. I'm going to go for a swim to clear my head and then write down everything I can remember. I'm sure we must have missed something," Gabby said as she cleared the coffee cups off the table.

Michael walked Scotty to the door; James left to go back to the security room to check on the progress of the cyclone preparations.

Gabby swam back and forth until she was exhausted. She showered and made her way back to her apartment. On the way she remembered they hadn't found Lenni's phone on his body or at his home. Where was the phone? Did the murderer have it or was it thrown from his body into the garden or down the cliff to the beach beneath? She called James to see if he had searched the grounds for the phone.

"No, I didn't search the grounds. I know we talked about the missing phone, but so much else was happening at the time I totally forgot to look around. Matt is on duty up there, let me call him and ask him to do a sweep of the grounds before the weather turns nasty."

Half an hour later, James called Gabby with an update. "Hi, Ms. Saintclaire. Yes, he found the phone; it was in the garden bed near the pool. The glass face is smashed, but it is working. Matt could tell me the last call Lenni received was a call from Susan Olsen at midnight; the call was seven minutes long. In fact, there have been many calls to and from Susan Olsen. His phone has had a lot of activity over the last few days, so I'm going up to his property to get the phone. I'll be back soon."

"James, who was it that told us Susan was having an affair with Lenni?"

"Kathy O'Connor told me that when I interviewed her over the phone."

"Thanks, James. I'm going to call Kathy and see if she can give me any more info about the affair," Gabby added.

Gabby picked up the phone; she flicked through the Rolodex to find the number to the supermarket. It was answered immediately and she was put through to Kathy without question.

"Kathy, it's Gabby Saintclaire from the resort. Can I ask you a couple of questions regarding Lenni's party? I understand you were there." Gabby waited for a reply.

"Actually, I'm going on my break, can I talk then? I'll be at Rosie's in ten minutes if you'd like to join me?" Kathy replied.

Gabby grabbed her coat. The wind was getting strong, the rain lashed around her as she ran for the car; thankfully the thunder had subsided for the moment. Assessing the situation, she decided it was safe enough to drive to the café. Of course, the next twelve hours would be a different story altogether.

Kathy had just put her order in when Gabby joined her at the table overlooking the supermarket. Gabby declined the offer of coffee. She wanted to get the conversation flowing so she could get back to the safety of the resort.

"Kathy, I wonder if you can tell me what you saw and who you talked to at Lenni's party. I understand you have already spoken to James."

"OK, let's see. We picked up Dwayne Olsen, and as none of us had been to one of Lenni's parties, we didn't really know what to expect.

I was amazed at how many people were there; Dwayne knew most of the young ones because of his footy coaching. I left the boys to drink and talk footy, and wandered outside to the pool.

I stopped to talk to Zara and Adam. They asked why I had brought Dwayne, what with Susan and Lenni having an affair. Then they realised I didn't know; they thought everyone knew, they even thought that was what brought on Dwayne's heart attack.

I assured them I didn't know and neither did Dwayne. I protested it must be a lie, but Adam said he was Lenni's gardener and he had photographic proof of them having it off in Lenni's bed—seems they forgot to close the curtains. It was Susan alright, he showed me the photo." Kathy stopped long enough to eat half her sandwich and slurp her peppermint tea.

"It was like being hit in the chest with a mallet. I felt totally defeated. What was I supposed to do with that information? I was shattered.

"Would I tell Dwayne, could I tell Dwayne? What if I didn't tell him, and then he found out I knew? I was damned if I did and damned if I didn't.

"So, I decided to tell him. I knew it would shock him, but I also knew he was going through a rough time at home and he wanted answers. Of course, this was what he was looking for, even though he probably didn't want to know it."

Gabby allowed Kathy to eat more of her sandwich and finish her cup of tea before it went cold.

"Kathy, how did he take the news?"

"Surprisingly well, actually. He had a couple of beers and then went to chat up the twins, Faye and Faith. He disappeared with them for a while, but he was OK when he came back. We drove him home and he was OK. I don't think he was angry or mad, just relieved.

"Was Susan at the party?"

"No, I didn't see her there, but her car wasn't at their house when we dropped Dwayne off, so I'm not sure where she was. Dwayne told us she was working, but he probably questions that now."

"Finally, Kathy, what time did you leave and who

was still there?"

"Gosh, I'm not sure of the time, I think it was around eleven, but can't be exactly sure. I don't really remember who was still there; I didn't see the twins after Dwayne came back. I know the rooms were relatively full when we arrived, but there weren't many around when we left, just not sure who. I wasn't really paying attention. I was more focused on Dwayne and how he was." Kathy spoke apologetically.

"That's fine, Kathy. You've been a great help, and I appreciate you taking the time to speak to me." Gabby hugged Kathy as she gestured to leave.

CHAPTER TWENTY-FOUR

Infidelity

All the way back to the resort Gabby was trying to think about the type of person Dwayne was. Why didn't he lash out when he found out his wife was having an affair, wouldn't that be a normal response? Something didn't feel right. She knew she would have to dig deeper to find out why Dwayne had accepted this infidelity so easily, and where was Susan if she wasn't at home and wasn't with Lenni? What would a real estate agent be doing working at 11:00 p.m. on a Saturday night?

Gabby voiced her concern to Michael when she got back to the apartment.

"I may be able to help you with that," Michael responded. "I saw her here at the resort that night. Remember, I got called to Mrs. Thompson's room as she was suffering chest pains. While we were waiting for the doctor to arrive, I noticed Susan going into the room next door. Find out who the guest is to the left of Mrs. Thompson and you may find your answer," Michael shrewdly replied.

"You're a lifesaver, sweetheart; you may have solved one of my problems." With that, she gave Michael the biggest kiss ever.

Gabby rang front reception. "Joan, it's Gabby, can you tell me who the guest is in the room to the left of Mrs. Thompson, and how is she by the way? Do we have an update on her condition?"

"Mrs. Thompson was discharged from the Medical Centre the next morning; it was just an angina attack. I personally picked her and Mr. Thompson up from the Medical Centre and brought them back to the resort. I made sure she had all the medications she needed and I called in on her before I finished my shift; she's fine. The guest to the left of her is a Mr. Grant Woodham. He's a frequent flyer here at the resort; you've probably seen him around. I know he's a property developer, but I'm not sure why that would bring him here to the island so often. To be honest I've never asked him, he's not very talkative."

"Thanks, Joan, much appreciated. Can you send a basket of fruit to Mrs. Thompson from the resort please?"

"I've already done that, and she was so thrilled with it that she wrote a lovely post on Trip Advisor," Joan responded.

"What would I ever do without you, Joan? You're amazing." Gabby was filled with pride as she hung up the phone. It was reassuring to know her staff was doing what they do best—looking after the wellbeing of the guests.

"Hey, Michael, have you met Grant Woodham around the resort?" Gabby asked.

"I've heard the name, but not sure if I've met him. Do we know what he looks like? Maybe I've been introduced to him; if I knew what he looked like I'd be able to tell you."

It didn't take long for Michael to recall the conversation with Roger Jackson, owner of Clairemont Resort. "Gabby, do you remember what Roger said about that property developer—he was doing a property deal with Lenni? I haven't heard anything about any new development on the island, have you?"

Gabby responded with a shake of the head, but then suddenly asked Michael: "I wonder if that is why Susan was meeting with Grant Woodham? Do you think her real estate agency is in on the deal as well? If the deal was a bit suss, that would certainly explain why they were meeting here in his room, as opposed to meeting in her office, wouldn't it?"

The sound of the phone broke Gabby's concentration. "Ms. Saintclaire, Joan here. I'm not sure why you enquired about Mr. Woodham. I'm wondering if he's complained about not being able to get off the island. He's been down a few times over the last couple of days, demanding to get off the island. I've tried to reason with him, but unfortunately, all transportation was fully booked and of course now they've cancelled all ferry crossings. I've explained he's here till after the cyclone, but he won't accept it and tells me I have to find another way. Is there anything I should know?" Joan asked.

"Thanks for the heads-up, Joan. Leave it to me. I think I'll go and see him. There are a couple of questions I want to ask him anyway."

"Michael, can you come with me to Grant's room? I'd like to explain we have done everything possible to get him off the island before the cyclone, but unfortunately, he's here for the duration. I also want to find out what this development is all about. Do you think we need to get James to join us?" Gabby asked for reassurance.

"It wouldn't hurt to have James there if he starts to get heavy about getting off the island. It might just stop him from doing something he may later regret. I'm intrigued as to why he desperately wants off the island—why the urgency." Gabby was pleased to see that they were both thinking the same thing, and James certainly agreed with them as they voiced their concern while walking to Grant's room.

Grant Woodham answered the door after the second knock.

"Hello, Mr. Woodham, I'm Gabby Saintclaire and this is my husband Michael, we are the managers of the resort and this is James Jollyman, our head of security. May we please come into your room?" Grant grudgingly moved to allow them to enter.

They heard a woman crying from the bedroom. James moved toward the door, glancing toward Grant as he did so. He opened the door to reveal Susan Olsen lying on the bed, crying her heart out.

"Ma'am, are you OK? Have you been hurt?" James inquired before proceeding closer to her.

"I'm fine, just upset." She sobbed out the words.

"May I ask what you are upset about?" James continued to take control of the situation. Knowing that Gabby and Michael were next door with Mr. Woodham, he started questioning her, to find out what was going on. It may just be a domestic, but somehow, he didn't think so.

"What do you want?" Grant demanded. "This is not a good time, you can see my friend is upset, please leave," he demanded again.

"Mr. Woodham, I have been informed from front reception that they have done everything they possibly can to organise transport for you off the island, but every mode of transport is completely full. There is nothing else we can do I'm afraid.

"You don't understand. I have to get off now, I can't wait till after the cyclone," Grant shouted.

Gabby, wanting to take the level of the conversation down a peg or two, tried to lower the volume with her voice. Compassionately and quietly she asked, "Mr. Woodham, why do you need to get off now, what is the urgency?"

"It's none of your business; I just have to, that's all," Grant shouted back at her.

Each time he spoke, Susan bawled harder and louder, even James had stopped trying to console her.

Trying a different tactic, Gabby enquired. "Mr. Woodham, it has come to our attention that you have been talking to Lenni Maxwell about a property development, is that correct?"

"That's none of your business either, why would you want to know about that?" demanded Grant.

Obviously, she had hit a sore point. "Mr. Woodham, are you aware that Lenni is dead? Do you know anything about that?"

Grant was totally speechless. Only the high-pitched wailing in the next room was heard as he slowly crumpled into a chair.

"OK, yes. I was in talks with Lenni, he was all for

the development, but last week he said he was pulling out. A billion-dollar deal that was signed sealed and delivered, and then he wanted to pull out. I came here to talk sense into him, that's all."

"And now he's dead—what do you know about that?" Michael asked.

"Nothing, honest. I know nothing about his death," Grant yelled.

Susan screamed through her sobbing tears, "NO, NO, NO. Not dead. Not Lenni. Tell them the truth, you lying bastard, just tell them the truth," she sobbed as she struggled to get the last words out.

CHAPTER TWENTY-FIVE

Revelations

Gabby walked into the bedroom: "James, can you please call for backup. I want to arrange for Susan to go to my apartment. I'll speak to her there."

Gabby left James to make the arrangements then she went back into the lounge and sat opposite Grant. "Grant, start at the beginning and tell me exactly what happened on Saturday night."

A very defeated Grant Woodham explained to Gabby, Michael and James exactly what happened— what had led to Lenni's death. Feeling satisfied with his response, Gabby allowed James to handcuff him and take him into custody. He would stay in supervised custody until they could find somewhere more secure to hold him.

Gabby, Michael and James made their way to their apartment to find Susan had composed herself. "Susan, sorry to put you through this, but we really need to know what happened on Saturday and what you know about Lenni's death."

"I understand." Susan took a deep breath and explained that Grant had called her at the office to come over to his room where he revealed that Lenni had pulled out of the deal.

"How could Lenni do that, we would all make millions from the deal. I know the money wasn't important to him, but he loved the condos and he was really into the deal. I didn't understand. So I called him to meet up. I forgot he was having a party. He wanted me to come over immediately, which was a surprise because he usually didn't want anyone to know about our secret meetings.

"He was drunk, I could hear it, and he was slurring his words. God knows what he was on, he sounded terrible. But I went over to his house. I saw a couple of people passed out in the lounge as I walked outside to the pool. That's where he always hung out. I didn't even think to look inside the house."

Susan stopped to gather her thoughts. She kept rubbing her hands over her legs as if trying to wipe something away and you could tell it was aggravating her. Her expression, unlike anything Gabby had witnessed before, was evidence she was reliving the event.

"There was nobody out by the pool when I got there. Lenni was passed out in his chair, so I tried to wake him, but he was almost incoherent. He eventually realised I was there and he thrust me in his lap where he violently raped me—it was terrible.

"I struggled with him, trying to break free. It was like he was possessed—he had the strength of a mad man; he held me so tightly I could hardly breathe, even though I was screaming at him to stop. I was hitting him with all my energy, but I couldn't break his grip on me. And then from behind I could feel someone trying to pull us apart. I know the chair Lenni was in hit the ground so hard it knocked him out cold.

"I knew the arms around me trying to protect me were Grant's. He must have followed me. He kept asking me if I was OK, but I was in shock. I couldn't believe what had just happened. He started dragging me away and it was then that I saw the blood on the ground.

"Grant sent me back to the resort. He told me to wait for him there, and he said he would take care of Lenni. I waited for ages and eventually he came back, saying everything was OK, that it was going to work out exactly as we wanted. We could go to Bali immediately and start our new life, and he would finalise the deal from there." Susan started sobbing again, at the realisation of what had just unfolded.

"Did Grant kill Lenni?" Susan asked through choked sobs.

"No, I don't think so, but we have to wait for the post-mortem. I think it was an accidental death. Grant has told us the same story, but he added that he couldn't find a pulse and realised the fall must have killed Lenni. But, instead of reporting it to the police, he threw his body into the pool and cleaned up the blood spill. He tried to make it look like he'd fallen accidently, but then realised just how foolish that would have been. He has admitted to us that he tried to alter the evidence, and he will be charged for that.

"What about me, will I be charged as well?" Susan asked.

"I'm not sure; you didn't actually commit a crime. You were an innocent bystander, so to speak, and I don't believe you actually knew Lenni was dead until now, so I don't think so. Obviously, I would recommend you speak to a lawyer, just to make sure.

"Susan, is there someone we can call, your husband perhaps? Does he know of your involvement with the property development?" Gabby wasn't too sure whether there was anything else going on with Susan and Grant, or with Lenni, other than the property deal, and it wasn't any of her business.

"No, I don't think that's a good idea. After this, I don't think I can go home, and I'm not even sure my business will survive the media fallout this is going to cause. I think I'll have to move to the mainland—try and pull myself together and start again," Susan admitted.

'Then can we offer you a room here for a few days? It's too late to get off the island now, and I imagine you will need some time to get yourself sorted and figure out if that's what you really want to do," Gabby offered.

"Thanks. That would be wonderful. My lawyer is on the mainland, I'll call her. I know I'm going to have to testify about my involvement in this crime, so I'd better find out where I stand before I make any more decisions."

Gabby walked Susan to front reception to organise a room for her. After showing Susan to the room, she called in to see James to get an update on Grant.

"Ms. Saintclaire, I have spoken to Mr. Anderson, he said the meeting with Ms. Robins went really well, and he may be able to retain his licence. Ms.

Robins called a few people and it was agreed that Troy could sit for the bar again, she would set it up upon her return to Melbourne. In the meantime, because of the cyclone Ms Robins is with him as they speak to Mr. Woodham and they are still in talks in the meeting room, a guard is on duty outside the room, and will continue to guard him until we can hand him over to mainland police.

"I tried to call D.I. Katrina Reid, but we have just lost communication with the mainland. Apart from getting written statements from Mr. Woodham and Mrs. Olsen, there's not much else I can do now except keep a close eye on him."

As Gabby walked into front reception, she noticed Joan was dealing with other guests who had unfortunately left the decision to get off the island till it was too late. She realised it was Stan and Rita Anderson. No wonder they want off the island she thought to herself. Troy had confided in Gabby about his agonising meeting with his parents.

The term *disowned* was never mentioned in his recollection to Gabby, but Troy's demeanor certainly spoke volumes. Troy was thankful that Rose had declared her undying support for him whatever happened next, and that was all he needed to move forward.

Regardless of what the heavens throw at us tonight, Clairemont Island is the best place to live and this is the best resort in the world.

I love my job, Gabby thought, knowing full well it was true.

As she recalled the feeling of turmoil that flooded her upon waking this morning, she was thrilled to acknowledge the eruption had been nowhere near as bad as what was now happening outside, but regardless of the impending cyclone, she couldn't wait for the next exciting drama to unfold on the island.

"A good man or woman will be honest
no matter how painful the truth is.

A coward hides behind lies and deceit."
Unknown

Trust The Universe

In *Trust the Universe* Vicki reveals how she dismissed intuition, gut instincts and messages 'from above' as she believed the messages she was receiving were so far-fetched they couldn't possibly be true.

But the Universe had its own plan for her and kept opening doors and connecting her to people of influence, until the 'slap in the face' the Universe was giving her could no longer be ignored.

What happened next became a catalyst for change; one by one circumstances occurred that would ultimately bring about an unbelievable outcome.

This book takes you on a personal journey and is just one example of what is possible when you let go of fear-based practices; when you believe in yourself and *Trust the Universe*.

Memory Of Your Life

Memory of Your Life is a step-by-step workbook designed to share your life stories with loved ones.

This simple, easy-to-use workbook gently guides you through life's most important memories and helps you record and share them in fine detail with poise, passion and purpose. It gives you opportunity to write anything left unsaid and give insights into the real you.

When Vicki began showing people this step-by-step workbook concept it became evident that many people resonated with it, they felt the same way, and it identified the need for a platform, like this workbook, to encourage people to record their stories and share them with family and friends.

A Deathly Shade Of Passion

A Deathly Shade of Passion is the second in the Clairemont Island Mystery series.

Tension builds when a magazine crew arrives from LA for a photo shoot. Having to source local talent seems easy at first. One person's life depends on their secret being kept under wraps, however a chance encounter brings past crimes into the spotlight.

The heady mix of L.A personalities and locals ignites a whole storm of passion and intrigue.

Around them, all hell breaks loose when pride and ego erupt causing a catastrophic outcome.

Some of the fascinating, scheming and wild characters from Deadly Deception appear here in a menacing romp through an increasingly sinister paradise.

About the Author

Author of Trust the Universe

Author of Memory of Your Life

Author of Deadly Deception

Author of A Deathly Shade of Passion

New Zealand born Vicki Williams lives in Australia. Vicki has always had a passion to write, but lacked the confidence to do anything more with her stories. That was until she entered a challenge to write a book in forty hours and shocked herself by producing her first book *Trust the Universe*.

Vicki has successfully taken other authors from story conception to publication as she mentors and teaches 'How to Write' workshops in person and online.

Vicki continues writing the Clairemont Island mystery series, as well as a young adult series written under the pen name of Jade Green. With a drawer full of possible storylines, it will be interesting to see where she leads us in the future.